LeROY, US MARSHAL

No matter what the odds, US Marshal Alvin LeRoy always completes his assignments. That's why he's been sent after the Reno gang. His pursuit takes him across southwest Texas, where he faces up to bushwhackers and the aftermath of a massacre as he relentlessly deals with the baddest bunch he's come across in quite a while. A trail of deception and danger ultimately leads him to New York, where he confronts the menacing top man of the crime syndicate who's behind the whole affair.

NEIL HUNTER

LeROY, US MARSHAL

Complete and Unabridged

LINFORD
Leicester

First published in Great Britain in 2017

First Linford Edition
published 2019

A catalogue record for this book is available
from the British Library.

ISBN 978–1–4448–3979–1

Published by
F. A. Thorpe (Publishing)
Anstey, Leicestershire

Set by Words & Graphics Ltd.
Anstey, Leicestershire
Printed and bound in Great Britain by
T. J. International Ltd., Padstow, Cornwall

This book is printed on acid-free paper

Liam Yarborough slouched from the cabin, looping his suspenders over his beefy shoulders as he made his slow way to the pump. Working the squeaking handle, he encouraged a gush of water and ducked his head under, gasping as the chill water sluiced down. He caught some of the water in his free hand and sucked it up into his mouth. Scraping his hand through his thick hair, he shook his head, spraying water like a dog emerging from a pool.

When he figured he'd done enough cleansing, he let go of the pump handle, straightened up, and took a long, slow look around. Not that there was much to see. Just a few scrubby trees, scatterings of thorny brush, and grass that had turned brown under the constant heat. To the far south, the hazy peaks of low hills, not high enough to be called mountains, broke the horizon.

There was a lean-to next to the cabin and a corral holding a single horse. The cabin itself was unusually large, a build of logs with a sod roof. A crooked chimney poked up through the roof, smoke curling in lazy spirals into the hot air. The windows were simply square-cut holes fitted with shutters on the inside.

The previous owners of the cabin were long gone. A family wiped out by a roving band of Quahadi Comanche making a final sweep of the Texas territory. At the time, the Comanche were on their last foray, their numbers heavily reduced by long years fighting the whites who were aided by the military. Whatever the hostiles hoped to achieve, it was a pyrrhic victory; and shortly afterward, the Comanche had been chased, hunted down, and finally taken captive by the army.

The cabin stood empty for a number of years until it had been taken over by the current occupants, one of them being Liam Yarborough. He was a member of the outlaw bunch led by Jack Reno, and would have been with them now if he hadn't been recovering from a couple of cracked ribs that made riding unbearable. Yarborough had taken Reno's advice to remain at the isolated cabin while his injury repaired itself. He didn't favor the idea, but even he had to admit his condition would have held the rest of the bunch back. So he consoled himself with knowing there was a substantial supply of whisky and food stored at the hideout. The bunch had been gone for close on three days, and Yarborough was starting to become restless, bored with his own company, and indifferent even to the cache of bottled whisky on hand.

Liquor had its drawbacks. Mainly it gave him a headache, lingering after a restless night's sleep. Yarborough figured dousing himself under the pump might ease the unpleasant sensation, so he'd done just that. The shock of the cold water drove away the fog of sleep but failed to lessen the dull ache inside his skull.

Yarborough rubbed a hand across his stubbled jaw. He hadn't taken a razor to it for some time. He was considering whether to shave when he sensed movement behind him and turned to see a black-clad figure, mounted and cradling a rifle across his saddle. The rider had eased quietly into view from behind the cabin, coming around the edge of the corral. It came as a shock to Yarborough as he realized the rider had come up unheard and unseen. He took a long look at the newcomer, certain he should know him; and when recognition did come, Yarborough dropped a hand to his side before he remembered he wasn't wearing his gun.

'Sonofabitch,' he said.

In all of the square miles of nothing, the mounted man had found him. He had ridden up to the cabin and caught Yarborough without a gun to defend himself. Yarborough called himself all kinds of a fool, his gaze flicking back

4

and forth as he searched for a way out.

The cabin door was ten feet away. Insignificant under normal circumstances, but right now it could mean the difference between life or death. Yarborough realized that, and also that getting to the cabin offered a possible chance. Slim as it was, Yarborough had to take it.

He saw the Winchester rifle lying across the rider's saddle. Not pointed at him, but close enough.

The difference between life and death.

Thin, but at least a chance.

Yarborough took it.

*   *   *

The moment Yarborough broke for the cabin, US Marshal Alvin LeRoy dropped his hand to the Winchester and lifted it. Fast as LeRoy was, Yarborough gained the advantage, twisting his body round and aiming for the cabin door. The thought crossed LeRoy's mind that he should have fired the moment he laid eyes on the outlaw. But it was simply a thought, quickly forgotten because he hadn't open fire, so it didn't matter.

LeRoy heeled his horse into motion, bringing it around the corner of the corral, his gaze on Yarborough's moving figure, the Winchester snapping into position. The shot was loud in the empty silence. The .44–40 lead slug took a long splinter out of the door frame as Yarborough went through, his shoulder slamming against the post as he vanished from sight.. It had been simply a warning shot, not a killing one.

LeRoy swung out of the saddle, pushing his horse to the side. He worked the Winchester's lever and put a fresh cartridge into the breech, moving around the corner of the corral, aware he had lost the advantage for the moment. It didn't put him off his stride. LeRoy was committed to whatever action it took and wouldn't allow himself to be distracted.

He flattened himself against the wall, the door to his right. He could hear frantic sounds coming from inside the cabin. That would be Yarborough searching for a way out. There was only one, through the door. The cabin didn't possess any additional doors or windows save for the ones at the front. The man had no other means of escape. He could stay where he was, but LeRoy was not going anywhere.

LeRoy realized that Yarborough's partners might show up at any time, though he would deal with that if and when it happened. He would handle matters as they occurred, as he always did, and today was no different.

*   *   *

With a strong-boned, not unhandsome face, his upper lip holding a thick dark mustache, LeRoy stood a shade under six feet tall, his good shoulders and torso above a lifelong rider's waist and hip leanness. He was dressed in black

7

pants and shirt, with a black vest that held his US Marshal's burnished badge. A wide-brimmed black hat and his black leather rider's boots, normally well-shined, held a patina of dust from his long ride, as did all his clothing. In addition to his rifle, LeRoy wore a .45 caliber Colt Peacemaker holstered on his right hip, and a recently added second Colt was fixed to his gunbelt, left side, butt forward; a backup weapon that gave him extra firepower. In a separate leather scabbard on his horse's right side sat a cut-down Parker Brothers side-by-side double-barreled 12-gauge shotgun. It might only have a short range, but the presence of the weapon in his hands was a sure way of curbing most men's violent tendencies. The concentrated effects of its twin barrels, throwing out a deadly burst of lead shot with tremendous power, was a crowd-stopper. LeRoy had seen the results the Parker produced and they were not pleasant.

When it came to using his firearms,

Alvin LeRoy gained an advantage over his opponents. He never hesitated once a situation reached the critical point. His commitment was absolute. He understood the need to take his shot before the man facing him. If he paused, he allowed the other man to make his move; and once that was decided, his own life was at risk. LeRoy would never allow that to happen.

Over the years, his reputation as a dedicated lawman had been bolstered by that very fact. His record spoke for itself. He was strong-willed and totally honest in his dealings with those who broke the law. The country was young, and there was a wildness about the frontier that was seized on by the men who rode the outlaw trails. They saw bountiful advantages in those territories where the law was spread thin. Where there were riches in existence, there were those who saw the opportunities to take from the weaker. These men, driven by greed and lacking a conscience, used the gun to enrich their own lives. By violence, they took what they wanted and shrugged off any kind of responsibility.

Alvin LeRoy had worn a badge from a relatively young age, moving from deputy sheriff to full-time lawman, and his growing reputation as a force for upholding the law had brought the offer to join the US Marshal service. LeRoy never looked back. Pinning on the badge was the best move he could have made, and over the intervening years the name LeRoy became synonymous with the profession. Some called him overly strict in his dealings with lawbreakers, a criticism that LeRoy simply ignored. He worked by the book and viewed those who brushed aside the law in order to further their greedy ambitions as a blight on honest people. His job was to pursue lawbreakers and bring them to justice. Killers who gunned down the innocent, however that was interpreted, had stepped beyond the bounds of civilized exist-ence and had no one to blame but themselves when it came to a reckoning.

LeRoy was no avenging angel. Where mistakes were made and realized, he was the first to step back and offer an apology. There was respect for LeRoy, albeit grudgingly given. Even those he stood up against would admit he never pushed himself over the limits of his authority. It could be a gray area, knowing when to stay his hand in any given situation, though LeRoy understood there were those individuals who would take advantage of any hesitation on the part of a lawman.

Liam Yarborough was the kind who would do just that. He was imbued with an animal cunning when it came to survival, and was never slow to make the most of a situation. He knew LeRoy was not the kind to gun down an unarmed man. Hard as he was, the lawman lived by a set of rules; and though they sometimes forced him to hold back, he would stay his hand if he considered they would compromise him.

Yarborough had considered LeRoy's position. The marshal had his man under his gun — yet that man was carrying no weapon, and Yarborough played on that fact. LeRoy had never fired on an unarmed man, so he took a gamble that paid off. LeRoy's shot had been a warning, a chance the outlaw might pull up short and raise his hands in surrender. Yarborough didn't, so LeRoy was left without his man for the moment. Liam Yarborough knew that was not going to last. He was briefly out of LeRoy's sight, but a long way from being free and clear. The lawman was still outside. Yarborough was left with no way out except the front door of the cabin; and the moment he held a weapon in his hands, all bets were off. He became a legitimate target. LeRoy's next would be no warning shot. He would fire with deadly intent.

★　★　★

Yarborough was fast becoming angry. Without warning, his peaceful situation had been turned around. Boring as it had been, Yarborough would have welcomed its return. Wincing against the surge of agony from his damaged ribs, he reached for his handgun, snatching it from the holster where his gunrig lay on the rough-hewn table. He checked the load. Five in the cylinder. He picked up a spare cartridge from the ones scattered on the table and loaded the empty chamber, then pushed the revolver behind his belt. Then he reached for the .44 caliber Henry repeater lying nearby. He knew it was fully loaded because he had spent time cleaning and reloading the rifle before he had gone outside. Despite his confining situation, he felt better holding the rifle in his hands, and let his rising anger spur him on.

'I know who you are, LeRoy, and it don't scare me none. You been dogging our trail for too damn long,' he said. His voice carried beyond the door of the cabin. 'Hear me, lawdog. I ain't afeared of you. You want me you come right ahead. 'Cause I got my rifle ready to blow you seven ways to hell.'

LeRoy allowed a tight smile to edge his lips. *Well, thanks for that piece of news.* 'Yarborough, it's not about to get any easier,' he said. 'You got no way out 'cept through this door, and I can wait. Sooner or later we got to settle this.'

'You got papers on me?'

'A bunch. And for the others. No easy way to say this, Yarborough. Time's running out for Jack Reno and his bunch. You boys pushed the score pretty high. Day's coming you got to pay. Figure it out; you might as well turn in your guns and take what's due to you.'

'Due? All I figure is a rope around my neck.'

'I can guarantee that. No chance of jail time for what you fellers done.'

'Then why should I throw down my guns and step outside?'

The hard sound of a shot broke the

14

stillness. The slug pounded the earth yards away. LeRoy stepped away from the doorway, sensing Yarborough was about to do something. More shots, each as loud as the previous one. He picked up a rush of sound: Yarborough making his break for freedom.

The man's bulk emerged from the shadowed doorway, his motion a blur as he cleared the frame, rifle swinging left to right, flame and smoke erupting from the muzzle. He was yelling, almost screaming, as if the noise would unnerve LeRoy. Yarborough's wild rush took him clear of the cabin, dust rising from beneath his boots.

'Put the gun down, Yarborough,' LeRoy said, his own weapon trained on the outlaw. 'Last chance.'

Yarborough came to a sudden stop, motionless for a couple of breaths, before he twisted around and faced the lawman. Sweat coated his face, and there was a wildness in his eyes as he stared at LeRoy.

'The hell with you, lawdog. No man's

15

going to put a noose around my neck . . . ' The Henry's long barrel came round, black muzzle searching.

LeRoy touched the Winchester's trigger. He felt the rifle jerk in his hands as a spear of flames erupted. The 44-40 slug hit Yarborough in the chest. The outlaw pulled back on the Henry's light trigger and sent a slug that burned the air close to LeRoy's cheek. The Winchester cracked a second time, and this slug hit an inch from the first, directly over Yarborough's heart. He fell back, mouth forming a soundless cry as he toppled and hit the ground on his back, the Henry jolted from his grasp as he landed.

LeRoy stood over the body, shaking his head. Yarborough had made his choice to go out fighting, most likely because he had seen no other way. The prospect of dying on the end of a rope was no alternative. He picked up the Henry and set it aside, then eased the walnut-handled 1875 model Remington from Yarborough's belt.

The single-action .45 caliber pistol looked to be in prime condition, the metal clean and holding a slight sheen of oil.

He made his way inside the cabin. The stale smell of sweat mingled with the tang of fried food as he stepped through the door. From what he could see, Yarborough and his companions were far from ideal tenants. The cabin's single room was strewn with clothing and scraps of saddlery. A collection of whisky bottles, some empty, others still holding liquid, covered the table. Stubbed-out cigarettes and cigars were littering the hard-packed dirt floor. LeRoy saw the empty gunrig Yarborough had left behind. Among the detritus left on the table were boxes of cartridges for rifles and pistols.

The smell of coffee teased LeRoy's nostrils, and he crossed to the pot-bellied stove that threw heat into the cabin. A coffee pot bubbled gently on the top. He located a tin mug and decided it was clean enough, filling it with coffee. He took sips of the hot brew as he wandered the room, not exactly sure what he was looking for.

He noticed a map tacked to one wall and took a long look at it, studying the pencil marks that had been made; and when he turned from the map, LeRoy had a smile on his face.

It wasn't much.

But it was a start.

★ ★ ★

Smoke from the burning cabin rose behind LeRoy as he set his horse on the southern trail. He had moved Yarborough's body inside, covering it with a blanket before dousing it and the cabin floor with the coal oil he had located. There was no way he could take Yarborough with him, or take the time to bury him, so he decided to give the man a cremation. Before setting the fire, LeRoy had freed the single horse in the corral and watched it break into a gallop once it was clear. The map pinned to the wall was removed and folded away into a pocket of his shirt. He took the Remington pistol and a couple of boxes of ammunition from the table and packed these in his saddlebags. Additional weapons and ammunition were not to be passed over lightly, though he left the Henry rifle leaning against the outside wall. The weapon was not one LeRoy favored. He preferred his Winchester. Outside, after setting the oil alight, he filled both his canteens with fresh water from the pump, mounted his horse, and rode away.

He didn't look back until he had covered a quarter mile or so. By this time the cabin was fully ablaze, and LeRoy could hear the sharp crackle of ammunition detonating from the heat.

This was in his second week trailing the Reno bunch across the desolate southwest Texas landscape. Liam Yarborough had been his first contact. That left Jack Reno himself, along with Hank

Malloy, Dixie Reed and Reeve Donnelly. The Reno bunch.

A hard-nosed collection of social misfits who were too lazy to work but figured the world owed them a living. Between them, they were responsible for numerous killings and a long list of money-oriented crimes. They were easy in their choices of venues. Banks. Stores that had cash registers to clear. Stagecoach strongboxes. Likewise, though distinctly harder to pull off, were trains carrying cash. Lower on the scale were simple holdups of individuals carrying money. Winners of hefty gambling pots, followed from a long session at the tables, had suffered the indignity of a gun muzzle poked in the ribs before being relieved of their winnings.

As bad as those events were, there was always the misfortune of being physically attacked during and after the theft. Violence was also a stock-in-trade of the Reno bunch, there being the thought that if a victim was set upon, it was going to be remembered by the next unfortunate who fell afoul of the bunch, so would generally reduce the possibility of anyone resisting in the future. In most instances it worked, but on occasion some hardy individual took exception to being robbed and fought back. That had been the case when Liam Yarborough had been attacked by a tough cattleman who had won a sizable poker pot. The bunch had stopped him on the way home, demanding he hand over the few thousand in his pocket. The man resisted, had pulled a gun and shot at Yarborough, cracking a few ribs before he took a number of bullets himself, which had been fatal. The bunch took the man's money and rode away.

A week later, LeRoy had shown up in the small town where the incident had taken place, the closest he'd gotten to the Reno bunch for some time, and took off in the hope he might be able to catch up with them. He trailed them steadily, aware he was a fair distance behind. LeRoy kept going, certain he would catch up with them in time and hoping he might close the gap before they carried out any further crimes. His dogged pursuit would eventually succeed; though when he did, he'd only come upon Liam Yarborough.

*　*　*

LeRoy rode until the light faded, then made camp in a cottonwood grove where a thin, clear stream meandered between the trees. After off-saddling, he tended to his horse. He gathered fuel for a fire, then heated water for coffee. He had some beef jerky in his sack. It was tough fare, but it would give him sustenance until he reached the next place where he could buy himself a decent meal. LeRoy had learned over the years to exist on small meals on the trail. He had beans in his possibles bag, but right now he didn't have the wherewithal to go through the motions of cooking them. He downed a number of mugs of coffee when it was ready, accompanying the hot brew with a cigar from the dwindling supply in his saddlebags.

After seeing to his physical needs, and before he settled down for the night, LeRoy took his weapons and gave them a wipe-over with a soft cloth he carried, checking the action of each and making sure they were all loaded. Even though he knew they were well cared for, it was a ritual he carried out regularly. In his line of work, his guns were often all that stood between him and injury or sudden death. Alvin LeRoy was not about to allow himself to fall into the trap of having his guns let him down. As an afterthought, he took the Remington from his saddlebag and gave it a thorough check. No point in having a spare weapon if it wasn't clean and ready for use. Once he had finished, he put the pistol, the hammer resting on an empty chamber, back in his saddlebag.

It had been a long day, so when

LeRoy wrapped himself in his blankets against the night's chill, sleep came quickly.

* * *

Laura Wakefield saw the group of horsemen even while they were a distance away. The flat Texas landscape they were crossing hid very little. When she first saw the four riders, their image shimmering in the heat waves rising from the baked earth, she imagined it was a mirage; one of those false images produced by the heat and given an ethereal projection. She passed a hand over her eyes, blinking against the brightness, expecting the images to vanish; but when she cleared her vision, the riders were still visible.

She hauled on the reins and pulled the oxen wagon to a stop. It creaked and swayed. Dry joints in the wood and on the wheel hubs made a slight noise. If she had told the Reverend Tamber once, she had told him countless times, but he always passed her advice off as merely the whining of a woman who should better know her place. After a time, she stopped making comments and simply drove the wagon. After all, she was only there to cook and clean, tend the stock, and keep her views to herself. Tamber, a self-proclaimed messenger who carried the word of the Lord, was the guiding light within the small group. As long as they did his bidding, he was content. If they challenged him, his rebukes came thick and fast; and no one, not even the men in the group, were willing to go against his authority.

Behind Laura, the other three wagons halted. Moments later, she heard the thud of hoofs as Tamber spurred his horse alongside.

'I gave no command to stop,' he said, staring at her with a grim expression on his angular, weathered face.

As always, he wore his black clothing, now dust-lathered and salt-rimed. The shadow from the stiff brim of his dark hat fell across his unsmiling features, and not for the first time did Laura wonder if the man ever smiled.

'Riders coming in,' she said evenly.

Early on, she'd realized that the way to stand up to Tamber was never to respond to his downright aggressive posturing. Unlike the other four women in the party, who cowered under his bleak authority, Laura refused to allow herself to be dominated. If anything, it made him even more determined to break her spirit. She had told herself many times that would never happen. Though she was only in her mid-twenties, Laura had faced hard times and she had survived. She had been down to her last few dollars when she had heard Reverend Tamber was seeking a woman who could cook and drive a wagon pulled by oxen, and who was willing to join his group as they crossed the Texan wilderness, taking the word of the Lord and a precious cargo to the settlement that had been established near the Pecos River. The journey would be a spiritual experience, according to Tamber, with the Lord's blessing and protection. Laura was less interested in those matters and more in the fifty dollars in cash and meals along the way that the work promised. The wagon she drove, holding food supplies and equipment, proved to be a tough job; but as Laura had dealt with an oxen team before, she handled it well enough to satisfy the reverend. He disapproved of her working attire — butternut pants and a check shirt, rawhide boots and a wide-brimmed hat to keep the sun off her. But Laura ignored his scathing looks, telling herself there was no way she could do the job clad in a dress and sun bonnet.

Tamber followed her pointing finger, screwing up his eyes as he studied the quartet of horsemen emerging from the distant haze and taking on corporeal form. 'Friendly travelers on the road,' he said, as if that answered all. 'They are brothers to be welcomed.'

Laura bit her lip. She could have said something, but decided it was too hot to engage with Tamber, so she didn't share her feelings. Now that the riders were closer, she could see they were all heavily armed; and there was something in their manner that told her they were far from friendly. She hoped she might be mistaken, but a feeling of apprehension settled over her.

Tamber, you're going to reap what you might try to sow, she thought.

The reverend eased his horse around the front of her wagon and set himself in the direct path of the four riders as they closed in. Up close, Laura's misgivings were compounded as she took in the stained, dusty clothing, the unshaven faces and the expression in their eyes as they set their horses in a loose line. They made no attempt to conceal their avaricious looks as they scanned the wagons and horses.

'Do you travel far, brothers?' Tamber said.

The obvious leader of the bunch, Jack Reno himself, hunched forward in his saddle, tipping his sweat-stained hat back. 'No damn need for that fool password now. We all know who we are and why we're here.'

Tamber nodded, recognition in his eyes. 'You've come earlier than was arranged.'

Reno managed a toothsome grin, twisting in his saddle to glance at his partners. 'Hell, yes, Parson. Damn right we found you. We been lookin' for you and your flock long enough. Been a hot ride. Too hot to waste any more time. Now show me where you got that package stashed away.' As he spoke, he let his right hand drop to the holstered Colt on his hip, drawing it slow and deliberate.

Tamber sensed an impending problem. 'No need for that, brother. I've kept my part of the bargain. Your goods are safe in my wagon. But this was not . . .'

From where she sat on her wagon,

Laura saw Reno's move, and fear clutched at her throat as she understood what was about to happen. She was about to call out a warning, but Reno's draw quickened and the big pistol leveled, hammer back, and spoke with a heavy blast of sound. The .45 lead slug hammered into Tamber's chest, tipping him back out of the saddle. Reno followed him as he fell and placed a second shot into his skull as he slammed to the dusty ground.

Smoke curled from the muzzle of Reno's weapon as Laura rolled across the wagon seat and threw herself clear. Even as she braced her fall with both hands, she landed hard. Panic began to seize her. She fought it back, scrambling to gain her feet. Without warning, she heard more gunshots — a rolling crackle of sound that mingled with yells of alarm and screams of terror. As she pushed upright, with no coherent thought as to what she was going to do, she heard the stamp of hoofs. They were closing in on her. As she turned around, a horse and rider loomed up in her vision. The man in the saddle was grinning as he brought up his gunhand, aimed the pistol at her and fired.

Laura felt something smash into her head, pain blossoming, followed by an overwhelming darkness that shut out everything, sight and sound; and she didn't even feel herself fall. Or feel the impact as she struck the hard ground . . .

★   ★   ★

When consciousness returned in a ragged, jumbled form, she had no idea where she was, for a while even who she was, as she lay motionless. The first real sense she regained was pain; a savage ache that was threatening to tear her skull apart. It frightened her, sickened her, her body alternately shivering, then pulsing with a feverish heat. Laura lay, scared to move, eyes closed because she was wary what she might see. Confusion crowded her mind, fragmented images all demanding attention.

The four horsemen appearing. Approaching the wagons.

Reverend Tamber moving to greet them. *I've kept my part of the bargain . . . your goods are in my wagon . . .*

The leader smiling. Lifting his gun and shooting Tamber.

And then her own panicked attempt to escape, the air full of screams and gunfire.

The rider looming over her . . . his face dominating her vision . . . the gunshot that delivered pain and then nothing . . .

. . . and now she was awake, struggling to make sense of it all. Fighting the hurt in her skull. The blinding pain that burned her very senses.

Then she was aware of the silence around her. A silence that was frightening in its intensity. An unnatural quiet.

The four riders were gone.

She knew she had to move; to get to some kind of cover. The sun shone hard overhead, burning through her clothing and searing her skin. Laura pushed up off the ground, hands against the gritty dust as she sat up, groaning against the persistent ache in her head. It took a while before her eyes focused and things took shape; but when they did, she wished she hadn't looked.

The wagon she had been driving was yards away, the ox team lying on the ground with bloody bullet holes in them. Turning her head, she saw the other wagons. All still. And the horse teams shot in their traces where they lay.

Then she saw the bodies. Every member of the party. Men, women, even the children. Sprawled on the unyielding ground, riddled with bullet holes, clothing stained with their dried blood. She sat for a long time, simply staring, struggling to understand the reason why. She felt tears form and spill down her face.

The simple question formed in her mind: *Why?*

What had generated the slaughter of

these people? By strangers who had appeared from the wasteland. Who had cut them down without pause.

Laura rose to her feet, swaying as a dizziness swept over her. She fought the sensation, refusing to let it claim her. Pushed back the nausea. She raised a hand to the left side of her head and felt the dried, crusted blood that covered her cheek; let her fingers move up until she felt the ragged wound across her skull. Her hair was matted with blood. She recalled the gunshot. The brutal pain as she had fallen. Her probing fingers found the long gash, the torn edges of flesh, still moist where she touched. Her fingers came away slick with blood. A moment of terror made her realize how close she had come to dying. Then her resolve asserted itself and she forced herself to take stock. She was alive. And she intended to stay that way. Whatever had happened, she had survived. She needed to face that.

She moved to her wagon and climbed up on the box, seeing the way the interior had been torn apart, and then searched beneath the seat for the wrapped bundle she kept there. It was still in place: a roll of thick cloth that concealed a heavy Remington .45 caliber pistol, along with a bundled leather holster and belt with filled bullet loops. The reverend had not approved of her displaying the rig, so she had concealed it under her seat. Not that it would have saved her from the guns of the men who had attacked the group. Holding it now offered a little comfort. The weapon had belonged to her deceased brother. It was the only possession he had, and on his death a few years ago Laura had kept it. Something to remember him by? Not that they had been overly close, but it was something. Every so often, she would take the gun and clean it; hold it before wrapping it up and putting it away again.

Back down off the wagon and feeling self-conscious, she put on the belt and holster, dropping the Remington into the leather. It lay heavy against her hip. Her gaze fell on the water barrel fixed to the side of the wagon. Seeing it made her realize how thirsty she was. When she went to it, she saw the ragged bullet holes near the base. Anger flared. The raiders had shot into the barrel, letting precious water drain away. Laura moved to the other wagons, checking the water barrels on each one. All had suffered the same fate, ragged holes where bullets had splintered the wood, allowing the water to drain away.

No water, no horses. Even though the wagon occupants had been killed, the raiders had destroyed the livestock and emptied the water supply. She tried to work out why they had done that. Some kind of perverse pleasure? A need for destructive action simply because they could do it? Too much thinking only increased the ache inside her head. Laura chose to check each wagon in case the attackers had missed any canteens that might have been kept inside.

She had to avert her gaze when she came into close contact with any of the dead. Seeing the children was the worst. Their bloody, sprawled bodies affected her the most, and she was unable to hold back the tears. This time she didn't even try.

She found a couple of filled canteens in one of the wagons, hardly believing her good fortune. A moment of guilt washed over her as she saw the dead bodies slumped beside the wagon. People she had known and talked to, even though it had only been for a short time. Her need for water overrode her misgivings, and she lifted one of the canteens and drank sparingly. She splashed more of the water on her face, letting it wash away the dirt that clung to her hot skin. She avoided wetting the wound on her head for fear of loosening the caked blood and starting it running again. Resting against the wagon, away from the dead, she took in more water.

Something was running around the

edges of her conscious mind. Only now, as she managed to concentrate her thoughts, Laura found herself making sense of it. An image of Reverend Tamber watching the four riders move in towards the wagons. The way he had reacted to their appearance. Surprised. A little annoyed because they had shown up unexpectedly. Before they should have . . . Tamber's reaction to the riders.

And then the words she recalled. *I've kept my part of the bargain.*

Things fell into place.

Tamber had known the riders. Had expected them, but not as early as they'd arrived. Whatever arrangement they might have had was changed the moment the lead rider shot Reverend Tamber. Laura realized they must have wanted something from the train; something concealed in Tamber's wagon. Whatever it was had been valuable enough to kill for. And Reverend Tamber had known what it was, because he had been working with the killers, transporting an unknown object to a rendezvous with the four men; to a lonely spot where they could collect the item away from curious eyes and ride away with it, leaving behind the only witnesses dead and unable to tell the tale — including Reverend Tamber.

Only, they had failed to eliminate one witness. Left for dead, Laura Wakefield had survived. She had witnessed the whole scene. She had seen the faces of the four men and would be able to identify them.

Her first reaction was to snatch the pistol from its holster, dogging back the hammer as she raised the weapon. She found herself staring about her, for a brief moment imagining that the four riders had come back.

For her.

She was partially right. As she turned about, she saw a horse and rider appear out of the heat haze, moving in towards the wagons.

Not four riders . . . Just one. Moving

in her direction, a rifle canted across his saddle as he closed in.

★   ★   ★

LeRoy had picked up the wagon trail late in the afternoon. It had run parallel with the Reno gang's tracks. His first instinct told him this was simply a coincidence. The wagons had come in from a different direction but were now travelling in a similar one. It was entirely possible the train was the intended target of the Reno bunch; that the outlaws were about to meet up with it somewhere ahead with the intention of . . . attacking it? Wagon trains, for the most part, were not liable to be carrying much of value. Personal possessions, maybe. Reno went for money, so even if the train was carrying cash, would it be enough to satisfy the outlaws? If LeRoy was correct in his thinking, and unless Reno knew something he didn't, any meeting might turn out to be dangerous for the occupants of the train. With his previous record of using casual violence, the passengers might very well be in for a hard time.

LeRoy urged his horse to greater speed. He didn't favor overdoing it. In the harsh climate, pushing a horse too hard could be a foolish mistake. Yet something told him he needed to catch up with the wagon train. He was starting to get a bad feeling.

★   ★   ★

A rule Dixie Reed never broke was to ride in on somewhere without making certain it was safe to do so. That even applied to returning to the cabin unannounced and before it was decided it was clear. In all the months they had been using the place as their base, they had only once had a caller, and that had been someone Jack Reno knew. The man had come with information Reno had been waiting for. Despite the relative isolation of the cabin, Reno still treated it with caution, and always had one man on the lookout. Now, with Yarborough in place and keeping an eye on things, Reed still needed to be sure he was in the clear before riding in. Reno had sent him to collect Yarborough and bring him back to join up with the group. Yarborough was going to have to tough it out, regardless of his injured ribs. With the first part of the job done, Reno wanted Yarborough back with the rest of the bunch. With the wagon train and Reverend Tamber out of the way, he had decided not to return to the cabin, instead going directly to the rendezvous so he could complete the deal.

The lanky, gaunt-faced southerner, Reed, was the best man for the job. His tracking and scouting skills were the best in the group. He had proved it on many occasions, being able to creep up on an unsuspecting adversary unheard and unseen, getting in close enough to use the razor-edged blade he carried before his target realized.

On leaving the bunch and returning

to meet up with Yarborough, Reed had made a wide loop that, three hours later, brought him to the cabin from a different direction. Staying below the ridgeline of a low rise, Reed was able to see the blackened remains of the cabin below. No horse in the corral. The place looked totally deserted. Reed spent close on an hour observing before he moved in, swinging around the rear of the site, rifle at hand. He noticed tracks leading in from the east. A single rider. The trail of the single rider led away from the cabin. There was no doubt in Reed's mind that the rider was tracking the Reno bunch, and that led him to guess the man was some kind of lawman, or maybe some kind of bounty man. There were numerous handbills out on the Reno bunch, and the money offered for them dead or alive was slowly mounting up.

Reed rode up to the cabin, leaving his horse tied to the corral as he checked out the burned structure. The smell of charred wood held a trace of coal oil. And something else. The odor of burned flesh. It was something Reed had experienced before, and it had stayed in his memory. He found the charred remains of a body inside the shell of the cabin.

Yarborough? It had to be. He and Reed had been riding partners for a long time, as close as men could be in their situation. They had shared good and bad times, faced tough odds, and been forced to shoot their way out of a number of difficult spots.

'If I find him, I'll put in a bullet for you,' Reed said.

He went to his horse and mounted, picking up the rider's trail. If the newcomer stayed on track, he was going to meet up with Reno and the rest of the bunch eventually, and Reed wanted to be there when he did. Better still to meet him out on the trail . . . alone and without warning.

★   ★   ★

LeRoy had followed the tracks for half the day. He lost them a few times where the wind had scoured the earth, but picked them up again later. It was tedious work, made harder because he had to spend time bent over searching the dusty ground, and that didn't do his spine any favors.

'If I have to do this much longer, I'm going to end up with a damn hump. Just like that Quasimodo feller out of that book I read one time.'

The chestnut he was riding made a sound that might have been in sympathy, but LeRoy thought not. 'Hoss, you're no help.'

Mid-afternoon and LeRoy was ready for a break. The weather was hot, the air stifling, and he was sweating beneath his shirt. Sleeving his face, he halted the chestnut and eased himself out of the saddle, reaching for one of his canteens. He moved around to ease the kinks out of his spine, taking a small swallow to rinse out his mouth before he had a drink proper. He could feel the chestnut's eye on him and heard an impatient nicker.

'Now you got something to say.'

He tipped water into his upturned hat and let the horse satisfy its thirst. After a second mouthful of his own, LeRoy checked out the immediate area — and almost missed the flicker of movement as a single rider showed briefly a few hundred yards from his own position. The distant horseman eased back out of sight behind a ground hump. LeRoy stepped slowly back alongside the chestnut, hanging the canteen from the saddle, and with his back to the ground hump slid the Winchester from its sheath. He kept the rifle tight against his body as he walked around his horse until he had it between himself and the hump. He worked the lever to put a round into the breech.

'I seen you, feller. Now don't be shy, and we can dance whenever you're ready.'

He took the reins in his right hand

and walked the horse slowly, keeping the Winchester between himself and the chestnut. True, the bulk of his body was covered by his horse, but his head would be visible if the other man decided to take a shot. If the fellow was a marksman, he might make it, and LeRoy had to admit the thought was strong in his mind. In a situation such as this, however, a degree of risk was necessary. He wanted to draw the other man out. It was either that or make the attempt to mount up and ride out of range, which LeRoy didn't really favor. No matter how fast he might be climbing into the saddle, he was going to present an irresistible target.

In the end, the decision was taken out of LeRoy's hands. A gunshot tore apart the silence. LeRoy's horse gave a terrified shriek as a slug burned across its flank. It pulled away from LeRoy's grasp, bolting aside, still making a lot of noise, leaving LeRoy exposed. He froze for a couple of long seconds, his eyes alighting out the shooter as the man angled his lean body from full cover, his rifle swinging round as he picked out LeRoy. The Winchester in LeRoy's hands snapped into positon and he tracked his target, fired and levered and fired again a split second before the shooter triggered his own shot. A tug at his shirt told LeRoy where the other man's shot had narrowly passed. Then a puff of dust showed where LeRoy's first shot had hit over the man's left side. His follow-up shot cored into the man's chest, knocking him back and down.

As he saw the man fall, LeRoy moved in his direction, rifle lining up, and he put a third shot into the man's head, directly over his left eye. It was a final shot, the one that took the shooter out completely. The maxim was true that even a wounded man might still have it in him to make a final shot, but a dead man's hand was stayed for good. The shooter slammed back against the ground and lay still.

LeRoy walked forward, up the slight

incline until he was standing at the dead man's feet. He recognized Dixie Reed from one of the issued handbills for the Reno bunch. The man was known as a relentless killer, with little regard for human life. He was also known as a skilled tracker, LeRoy recalled.

'Not anymore,' LeRoy said.

He became aware of the irritating bullet sting where Reed's slug had left its mark. It had been close, but still a miss, he thought as he rubbed his hand across his side, feeling the seep of blood. He gathered up the dead man's rifle and slid his pistol from it holster, along with the long-bladed knife in his boot. He always felt comfortable when he removed weapons from an adversary, whether they were dead or not.

He returned to where his horse stood some yards off, restless and agitated. When he checked, he saw the bloody furrow Reed's shot had burned along the horse's right flank.

'Easy there, hoss,' he said. 'We'll doctor that.'

He continued to talk to the animal, stroking its neck and head, calming it down as he took torn cloth and a jar of salve from his saddlebags and wet the wound with water from his canteen before applying the salve.

'Be fine when the stinging goes away.'

LeRoy rein-tied the horse to a low bush and returned to where Reed lay, his corpse already attracting flies. He searched the man's pockets but found little of interest. Reed's tethered horse stood back in the brush and LeRoy crossed to it, unsaddled the animal, shucked its harness and then slapped it on the rump, sending it away. Next, he went through Reed's possibles and saddlebags. A few items of clothing. Extra ammunition. A bundle of dark cigars and a squat bottle labelled 'whisky.' LeRoy uncorked it and took a sniff, but the bitter smell was enough to deter him from taking a drink. He left everything except the cigars and the ammunition. Unfolding the blanket roll, he wrapped Reed in it and secured the makeshift shroud with lengths of cut saddle rope, then placed Reed's weapons inside the blanket alongside him.

Less than an hour later, LeRoy was back in the saddle, picking up on the faint trail he had been following before meeting up with the now deceased Dixie Reed. As he rode, he was working out in his mind the way things had transpired.

Reed had come to the cabin from a different route; and knowing the way Jack Reno's mind worked, he would have been sent ahead to see if their hideout had been discovered. The man had a survivor's way of thinking. He would have made sure he was on safe ground before he rode in, even if he was returning to a previously safe haven. He never took anything for granted, and always rode the cautious trail. It was most likely why he had survived for so long. The minute he had discovered the burned-out cabin, Reed would have searched around until he found LeRoy's tracks, seeing they were heading out along the earlier trail Reno and his bunch had cut. He had fallen in behind LeRoy, intent on cutting him down once he had him spotted.

And he had come pretty close to doing that, LeRoy had to admit. Close enough that it mattered. With that in mind, he had replenished the used ammunition in his Winchester before he slid the rifle back in its sheath.

The main thought in LeRoy's mind was that if Reed had been checking out the cabin, then Reno and his bunch could be on their way back as well. He would have to stay on the alert for any signs the outlaws were heading his way.

He recalled the place on the map he had seen on the cabin wall, circled in pencil. A deserted water tower along-side an abandoned railroad spurline. A man named Rufus Buckmann had sunk a great deal of money into the notion of building a line that would eventually connect with the main east-west tracks to bring more people to the area. Such a railhead junction would create a need for a town. There was the added attraction of the natural water supply that came from deep within the earth, creating a steady supply. With that in mind, Buckmann had marked out lots and driving wooden stakes into the earth, showing where buildings would stand.

However, Buckmann's dream never got further than his intended plan. It was a noble effort that had ended up being known as Buckmann's Folly. The enterprise had been a costly mistake. Problems had followed one after the other, and after repeated efforts to keep the project going, Buckmann had run out of enthusiasm and eventually money. Two months after the failure of the business, with his creditors closing in, he'd stuck a pistol under his chin and blown off the top of his head.

That had been five years ago. The

water tower, cabin, and rusted steel rails were all that was left of Buckmann's dream. The spring continued to flow, creating a shallow stream that watered the immediate patch of dry earth and allowed the already established greenery to flourish. The spot of watered earth attracted any who rode that way, becoming a drinking hole. LeRoy had ridden by the abandoned spot a number of times, never paying it much heed before, but right now it took on some significance.

He heeled his horse around and cut across the dusty Texas landscape. It was worth the ride to check out the location. LeRoy was thinking Reno was going to head for the spot, rather than return to the cabin. He was taking a gamble. If Reno and his bunch had chosen to visit Buckmann's Folly, they could have already been and gone. On the other hand, they might still be there, or possibly intending to visit. It was in the nature of his business to at least check it out. It was worth the ride, even if it proved to be a futile one.

A few hours later, he came down a long dip in the landscape, his destination still a fair distance ahead, and hauled his horse to a stop. Leaning forward, he studied the group of wagons sitting motionless under the hot sun. When he saw the ox team and the horses down on the ground, he slid his Winchester from the scabbard and held it close.

The wagon train from the tracks he had seen. It had to be.

Easing his horse forward, eyes searching, LeRoy rode in. The scene was unnaturally still. No movement. No sound.

Until a figure stepped into view from the far side, a raised Colt in one hand. A young woman, dried blood caking one side of her head and staining the front of her dusty shirt.

'You better have a good reason to be here,' she said. 'Make it convince me not to shoot you, because I can't miss from where I'm standing.'

LeRoy let his rifle lie across his saddle as he turned his body so the woman could see the gleam of his badge pinned to his shirt. 'LeRoy, US Marshal, ma'am. I mean you no harm. Truth be told, you look as if you could do with some help yourself.'

'Marshal, step down. You need to see this. I'm Laura Wakefield.'

LeRoy dismounted and followed the young woman to the other side of the wagons, where he was confronted by the multiple bodies. Hardened as he was to the grim sights he sometimes came across, he came to a shocked halt and looked over the men, women and children, at a momentary loss for any words to convey his feelings.

'I could have been one of them,' Laura said. She touched the side of her head. 'I took a bullet, as you can see. They must have thought I was dead. When I recovered enough to move, I was alone. This is what those men left behind.'

'Four riders?'

'How did you know that?'

'Been tracking them for a while. Jack Reno and his bunch. I dealt with two of 'em along the way. That leaves the bunch who hit you.'

'The Reverend Tamber was leading the group,' Laura said. 'Heading for the Pecos River, where he was to set up a church. People were waiting for him to arrive.' She paused in reflection. 'They'll wait a long time now. Marshal, Tamber knew those men. The ones who rode in. I heard the way he spoke to them, like he'd been expecting to meet them but not here. I didn't catch all that was said, but it was enough to know he was surprised. He . . . was still speaking when one of them pulled a gun and just shot him.'

The wanton killing didn't surprise LeRoy. It was Reno's way. Taking life meant nothing to the outlaw bunch. What did puzzle him was Reverend Tamber's involvement with them. A man of God mixed up with the likes of Jack Reno? It made little sense . . . unless Tamber was carrying something in one of his wagons that Reno wanted.

'Was Tamber transporting anything of value?'

Laura shrugged her shoulders. 'If he was, he kept it to himself. A few boxes of new Bibles. Prayer books and the like. Things for the church. He might have had some money he'd collected. Donations. But even that would have been a small amount, as far as I knew.'

'If Reno knew the man and rode out to meet him, it had to be more than that.'

'I heard Tamber say, 'I've kept my part of the bargain.' He had something hidden in his wagon. I heard him say that just before he was shot.'

'Interesting.'

LeRoy saw Laura sink to her knees, head down, a low sound escaping from her lips. As he moved to her side, she collapsed completely and lay still.

When Laura regained consciousness, she found it was dark. She was stretched out on a thin mattress from one of the wagons, a pillow beneath her head and blankets covering her. Daylight was fading. To one side she saw a fire burning, and she could smell coffee. She became aware of something around her head, and when she reached up she felt a wrapped bandage there. The ache inside her skull had lessened. Not exactly gone, but tolerable.

'Did what I could for that wound,' LeRoy said, appearing at her side. 'I found some medical supplies in one of the wagons. I'm no doctor, but I managed to clean you up and cover it.'

'I feel foolish falling down like that.'

'Miss Wakefield, you took a bullet to the head. I believe falling down is excusable.'

LeRoy helped her sit up before handing her a mug of coffee. She took it gratefully. The hot brew was strong.

'How long have I been unconscious?'

'A few hours. Rest was what you needed. I took the liberty of removing your old shirt and replacing it with a clean one. You spilled a considerable amount of blood down the old one.'

With all that had happened, having LeRoy partially undress her didn't seem important. 'Thank you, Marshal.'

'I prefer LeRoy.'

'Then you should call me Laura.'

'Food will be ready in a while. Nothing more than beans and hot biscuits.'

'What can we do about the bodies? Doesn't sit right, just letting them lie there.'

'I moved them. Covered them with blankets for the time being.'

Laura fell silent as memories of the people from the wagons came flooding back. She stared beyond the circle of firelight where the night hid the horror of death. 'That was good of you.'

A little time later, LeRoy handed her a plate of food, and despite the situation Laura found she was hungry enough to clear it. LeRoy hunkered down across the fire from her.

'What do we do now?' she said. 'Shouldn't you be going after those men? I'm holding you up, aren't I?'

'Let me worry about Reno and his bunch.' He dished out more food and refilled Laura's coffee.

'What those men did,' Laura said out of the silence, 'was the cruelest thing I've ever known. How could they — '

'Because it was the easiest thing for them to do. In their way of thinking, those people were witnesses. They could have identified Reno and his bunch. So they had to be removed.'

'LeRoy, there were children involved.'

'Youngsters have eyes. And remember things.'

'That's no excuse.'

'Those hombres don't need excuses. They see a problem they eliminate it.'

'They should be — '

'Their time's coming.'

Laura caught sight of his face in the

dancing flames of the fire. If the expression in his eyes was anything to go by, Jack Reno and his bunch were already riding their last trail. That look offered her comfort but also caused a shiver of fear to chill her spine.

Their time was coming.

* * *

LeRoy was still working on what to do with Laura the next morning as he built up the fire and fixed food and coffee. He had found supplies in the wagons and used them to provide breakfast.

It was the smell of bacon frying that attracted Laura's attention as she woke. She lay for a while, recalling what had happened the day before, slowly sitting up. Her head still hurt, though not as much as it had.

'Hungry?' LeRoy said.

'Yes.'

He plated bacon and biscuits fried in the fat, handing it to her as she joined him. Laura ate slowly, watching LeRoy as he poured coffee for them both.

'You know your way around a cookfire,' she said.

'When you spend as much time alone as I do, being able to cook is a necessity. Either that or you starve.'

'It must be a lonely way to live.'

'Can be if you allow it.

'Do you have a family somewhere?'

'Married sister in Albany is all.'

'You get to see her much?'

LeRoy shook his head and bent over his food. His reluctance to say more intrigued Laura. She had always been full of curiosity, though it sometimes brought her grief. 'Sorry,' she said. 'I didn't mean to intrude.'

'My sister and I don't get along well. Mainly because of my work.'

'As a lawman?'

'The part where I need to use violence. Martha doesn't approve of my having to use a gun.'

'If you didn't, you might be killed yourself. Can't she see that?'

'If only it was that clear-cut.' LeRoy

refilled his coffee cup. 'How did you come to be driving a wagon for Tamber?'

'He advertised for a teamster. I had experience driving an ox team for my uncle. Worked for him on his farm until he died suddenly. Some kind of fever took him. The bank reclaimed the farm to settle his debts, and I was left on my own. I heard about the job. Tamber was reluctant to take on a woman until I showed him I could handle his ox team, and then he changed his mind. It was going fine until . . . until those men showed up. You know the rest.'

'How old are you, Laura?'

She glared at him, her cheeks flushing. 'Old enough, LeRoy,' she said, her voice hard.

He pulled a cigar from his shirt and lit it with a sliver of wood from the fire. 'I was only making conversation.'

'I apologize. I'm twenty-five, and I guess by now I should be married with a family of my own.'

'We don't always get what we wish for.'

Laura sat upright, her head coming round. She put down her plate and cup. On her feet, she pulled the holstered Remington, easing back the hammer. 'Riders coming in. More than three.'

Standing close by her, LeRoy spotted the rising dust as a line of horsemen swung in towards their camp beside the wagons.

Uniformed men of the US cavalry. Dust-streaked and with unlimbered rifles in their hands as they converged on LeRoy and Laura Wakefield.

*   *   *

It was a small patrol of six men, led by a sergeant LeRoy knew. Lew Tolliver had more than ten years in the service. He had joined the army as a teen. His experience couldn't be bought; it came through those long years of campaigning against Indians and malcontents.

Gunrunners and whisky peddlers, killers and in general anyone who attempted to create problems in the territory. The hard-pressed army was there to help keep the peace, whether it was being aggravated by Comanches, though that danger was lessened now, or white outlaws and renegades. The frontier could still be a dangerous place. The settlers, in towns or on isolated ranches, were usually a long way from organized protection, so long-ranging military patrols did their best to offer what help they could. In many instances, communication being thin on the ground, any call for help was often too slow reaching the army. By the time any response came, the incident was over and often there was little to be done except bury the dead. It was not the army's fault. Military cutbacks created the situation where help was hampered by the lack of men and equipment. There was frustration in the military. Nothing they could do. They were at the beck and call of their political masters, in most cases hampered by men on the other side of the continent who in most cases had little experience in military matters and were too busy indulging in their own careers.

None of that helped the men having to police the vast territory under their control. To their credit, they performed to the best of their ability, and depended on the skills they had learned over the years.

Sergeant Lew Tolliver, as hard as the land he rode, was one of those men. Everything he knew had come from personal experience. Little came from books, because there was little that rules and regulations could teach a man about survival in the wilderness. Tolliver understood how to play the game. When to speak out and when to keep his opinions to himself, especially in front of his superior officers. There were those he respected, and some he wouldn't have trusted to fetch a pail of water from the well.

His patrol had been out for four days. Endless days under the merciless sun, eating dust and sweating beneath their wilting uniforms as they rode the endless terrain. In that time they had seen no one. Heard nothing. Boredom was fast setting in, and Tolliver was seeing the effect it was having on his squad.

So when the small wagon train came into view, even his jaded soldiers found their interest piqued. But seeing the dead livestock warned them of possible danger.

'Rifles at the ready,' Tolliver said. 'Eyes peeled, boys.'

They came in line abreast, allowing each man a clear field of fire if anything happened. Tolliver, slightly ahead, was the first to spot movement as a man stepped into view from the opposite side of the wagons.

'Sergeant Tolliver,' LeRoy said, lowering his own weapon.

Tolliver raised his hand and ordered his men to stand down. 'LeRoy, we always meet in the damndest places.'

A second figure appeared beside LeRoy. A young woman, dressed in pants and shirt, with a bandage around her head and holding a rifle she seemed to be ready to use.

'Laura Wakefield, this is Lew Tolliver, US cavalry. It appears we've been rescued by the army.'

'Do I take your word for that, LeRoy?'

Tolliver put his rifle away and ordered his men to do the same. 'Ma'am.'

'It's Miss Wakefield.'

'My apologies, miss. I was going to say we're here to help if we can.'

'A trifle late, Sergeant,' Laura said. 'I'll heat up more coffee.' She turned away and moved to build up the cookfire.

Tolliver turned and gave the order for his men to dismount and see to their horses. He slid out of his own saddle, passing the reins to the closest man. He stretched his legs, crossed to LeRoy and took the marshal's outstretched hand.

'What the hell's been going on here?' Tolliver was taking a long look around at the deserted wagons and the bloated carcasses of oxen and horses. 'And where are the folk belonging to this collection of wagons?'

LeRoy told him, leaving nothing out. Then showed him.

★ ★ ★

By midday, the dead had been buried, the cavalry troop under Tolliver's command digging graves and marking each family group with crosses constructed from wood taken from the wagons. Heated irons were used to burn some crude inscriptions into the timber. Laura had stepped in to identify the families. It had not been an easy task for her, but she summoned a reserve of strength to do it. One of the troopers carried a Bible with him, and they all stood around as he spoke words from it.

Laura, assisted by the patrol's nearest equivalent to a cook, used implements from the wagons and food from the supplies to prepare a meal, and the wearied cavalrymen sat down to eat.

'That woman has had to go through a lot,' Tolliver said. He stood with LeRoy, drinking coffee, watching Laura pass around the food. 'Has to be admired.'

'Lew, I want you to take her back to the fort. I've already spent too much time here. I need to get back on the hunt for Reno and his bunch. Put in your report and send a message for me back to my people about what's happened.'

'I'm not going to tell you you've got one hell of a job to tackle.'

'It's why I wear this badge, Lew. What I signed up for. I have to find those men. What they did here can't be ignored.'

'What if I send a couple of my men with you?'

LeRoy shook his head. 'No offense,

Lew, but they would hold me back. I work my own way. You know that.'

'Hard-headed as usual,' Tolliver said. 'You never change, Al.' Tolliver was one of the few men who used the shortened name and got away with it.

'I need to talk to Laura.'

'You need more food?' Laura said when he approached her.

'No. I need to speak to you.'

'Sounds serious.' She held his gaze, then said, 'You're leaving?'

LeRoy nodded. 'You know why. Tolliver will take you back to the fort. I have to move on.'

'LeRoy, I want to know why they killed all those people.'

'I'm guessing your reverend had something they came to collect. Like I said earlier, they wouldn't want witnesses after they shot Tamber. They didn't need him anymore. Remember, this is the Jack Reno bunch. They never leave anyone alive.'

'But women and children . . . '

'Laura, they don't care.'

'They used Tamber to move their . . . whatever . . . and decided he'd outlived his usefulness?'

'I'll let you know when I'm done.'

As he turned to leave, Laura touched his arm. 'I won't forget you. Take care of yourself, Alvin LeRoy.'

She watched him pause to speak with Tolliver before he mounted his horse and picked up the faint trail left by Reno and his men. He didn't look back, and she stood as horse and rider cut across country, finally vanishing over the hazy horizon.

★   ★   ★

LeRoy had a distance to cover. Reno had a good lead, but the lawman was confident he would catch up with them. The spot he'd seen marked on the map still in his pocket lay in the general direction the outlaws were riding. He was certain sure it was a rendezvous point.

Buckmann's Folly. Far enough out of

the way to arrange a meeting. That had been part of the reason Buckmann's plan had gone astray. His idea had been sound, but choosing the place had been his undoing. It wasn't the first time, nor would it be the last, a man had tried to leave his mark on the land and failed. The lure of striking the mother lode, whether land, or gold, or any other scheme, was endemic in the frontier. It was the reason men came seeking fame and fortune. Some succeeded while others did not. The West was strewn with the bones of failure. Rufus Buckmann had added his to that list.

The oppressive heat did not let up. LeRoy was sweating just sitting his saddle. His horse simply plodded forward, not entirely happy with the conditions. Dust rose in pale clouds around them, layering man and horse. He pulled out a neckerchief from his pants pocket, moistened it from his canteen, and tied it over his mouth. It wasn't an ideal solution, but it would do until he found something better. His horse must have smelled the water. It turned its head and eyed him accusingly until LeRoy drew rein and stepped out of the saddle. He poured water into his upturned hat and let the animal drink.

'Make the most of it,' he said. 'We don't have much to spare right now.'

LeRoy brushed his fingers through his gritty hair before he put his hat back on, feeling the welcome coolness the damp hat provided. He scrubbed a hand across his stubbled jaw beneath the neckerchief, thinking it would have been nice to settle in a barber's chair and let someone shave him. Come to that, a long bath and a change of clothes wouldn't go amiss. He dismissed his thoughts, however; they were for another time. After he had dealt with Reno and his bunch.

Hard men in a hard land, bred and molded by their environment. It took a special breed to survive in the harshest country. A man's spirit could easily be crushed by fighting daily challenges. Yet many did, refusing to bow down, and staying the course. They were taming a new land, and it took courage and determination. It was not an easy course, nor was it a victory won overnight; but the spirit of the people would allow them to overcome.

However, men like Jack Reno were of a different persuasion. They saw opportunities to reach out and take what other men worked to achieve. Vultures on two legs, waiting to swoop down and snatch away the rewards of hard labor.

Which was why men like Alvin LeRoy were around, sworn to uphold the law and wearing the US Marshal's badge. They chose to stand against the outlaws. But it was a thankless task; a life of lonely trails and danger, riding the empty miles in pursuit of men who would kill without thought, risking their lives for little reward.

In reflective moments, LeRoy asked himself why he did the job; why he stood in the firing line. His only answer was that he believed in the law; that he put up with it all because he felt it was the right thing to do. From the first time he had pinned on a badge, LeRoy had seen the need for law as a way to help keep civilized existence in check. He took to the job with a steady purpose, finding it gave his own life a line to walk. He came to see it was the way for him, and he never looked back.

★　★　★

LeRoy hauled back on the chestnut's reins, feeling the horse rear up, losing its grip on the loose slope. He tasted the acrid and gritty dust as it flew up from beneath the horse's hoofs.

Then he heard the first shots. The gun blasts were loud. Close. The chestnut gave a shrill squeal as it took a number of slugs. It plunged on a few more steps before it tumbled, tipping LeRoy forward in the saddle. He kicked his feet clear of the stirrups, knowing the animal was going down, and let go of the leathers. The chestnut's legs went from under it and it pitched violently forward. LeRoy rolled from the saddle, the slope unforgiving as he slammed into it. Lost in the swirl of dust, he rolled, sensing the heavy bulk of the stricken horse falling in his direction. It struck him shoulder high, the force of the impact cartwheeling him across the slope. With his breath driven from his lungs, LeRoy was helpless to resist. He bounced a few times, struggling to pull air back into his starved lungs, before he felt himself sliding down the slope, hands clawing at the surface in an attempt to stop his descent.

Dust formed a pale cloud around him, grit peppering his face and getting into his mouth. He picked up a raised voice. Then a second.

Sonofabitch.

The shooters would be closing in on him. The only protection he had was the dust rising around him, and that wouldn't last for long. LeRoy sucked air into his lungs, the sour taste of the dust threatening to choke him.

He made a grab for his holstered Colt on his right hip, pushing the hammer-loop free, and drew the weapon. He didn't touch his second pistol, leaving it for backup if he needed it.

You'd better do this right. There won't be a second chance.

LeRoy felt his right foot lodge against a solid shape jutting from the slope; a partially buried rock. It stopped his forward motion and he used that to twist his body round, sprawling on his back.

A shot came close on his left. He felt the impact as the slug pounded the slope inches away, and moved onto his side. Out the corner of his eye, he picked up the muzzle flash; a brief indication of the shooter's position. LeRoy turned his Colt that way, hammer back, and fired twice, each shot making a heavy sound. He heard a man grunt.

'Carson?'

The call came from his right, close

enough that he was able to make out the hazy shape of the second man moving into his line of vision. LeRoy swept his muzzle forward, triggering and firing off three fast shots that merged into one solid roll of gunfire. He saw the target stop, body arching back under the solid impact of the .45 caliber slugs. Sliding the Colt back into its holster, he reached across for his backup weapon.

LeRoy pushed to his feet, sleeving pale dust from his eyes, and checked the area. The drifting haze cleared and he picked out the downed men, bodies splayed motionless across the slope. They had died hard and fast, expecting LeRoy would be an easy target. Their mistake.

He checked each man, clearing the dropped weapons, and felt better when he had done so. Only one face registered with him. Bren Halsted. LeRoy recalled seeing a handbill on him that had been circulated by a law office from back east. Halsted had a number of suspected crimes behind him, though nothing had been proven. He appeared to have a good lawyer on his side. But there was no connection with Jack Reno that LeRoy knew of. Halsted's clothes spoke of money. They were quality; well-tailored and expensive. Yet Halsted was a town man, more used to city life than wandering the badlands. It seemed he had signed on to side with someone who had travelled all the way to Texas to do business with Jack Reno.

LeRoy knew he was making guesses based on what he had learned from Laura. There appeared to be logic there, based on the facts as he knew them. It forced him to wonder what Reverend Tamber had been carrying in his wagon that had generated Reno's extreme actions. Something with value enough to kill for. Gold? Cash? Something with enough value that it brought about wholesale slaughter. Whatever it was, it had LeRoy's full attention.

He reloaded, then worked his way up

the loose slope to check his downed horse. The chestnut was dead. LeRoy took his canteen and took a mouthful of water to get rid of the dust he'd swallowed before he took a full drink, then slid his Winchester from the saddle boot and retrieved his saddlebags, but was unable to free his possibles sack. He wet his neckerchief and wiped his face, trying to remove the clinging dust. Yards across the slope, he spotted his hat and picked it up.

He was starting to feel the effects of his tumble down the slope after his horse had gone down. Aches across his ribs and down his spine. It could have been worse, he considered. Like a bullet wound. He concentrated on his next move — to find the horses left by his attackers. They had to be somewhere close. The pair hadn't walked to find him.

It took him less than ten minutes to locate the pair of tethered animals in a shallow depression. They were standing motionless, hobbled with leather restraints. LeRoy looked them over. A sturdy gray and a sleek-coated black. The latter eyed him with a silent stare, showing its big teeth. LeRoy judged it to have a defiant spirit; an animal that would need a strong hand to keep it under control. It would be a resilient ride, and that appealed to him. LeRoy laid his gear down, topped his hat with water, and let both animals drink. There were canteens on both saddles, so he could spare the water, and he hung them from the saddle horn. Next he stripped off the gray's rig, unbuckled the hobbles, and set the animal free. After he checked out what supplies had come into his hands and selected what would be most useful to him with regards to food and extra ammunition, he swung his saddlebags in place, securing them. He took off the black's hobbles, keeping the reins in one hand as he freed the animal. The horse pulled away, and it took LeRoy a minute to calm it, talking all the time so it got used to his voice, and eventually it finally decided to stand.

'Now you got that out of your system, let's quit fooling around,' LeRoy said. 'We've got some travelling to do and I need you to settle down.' He stroked the glossy neck, feeling the ripple of muscle under his hand; and when he stepped up into the saddle, the black stood motionless. 'See, that wasn't so bad, son.'

LeRoy cast around, eyes on the ground, and it took him no more than a few minutes to pick up the tracks left by the two riders as they had ridden in. He put the black on the trail and began to retrace it.

'Well, son, looks like we're on our way.'

★   ★   ★

The tight group of men gathered around the derelict water tower at Buckmann's Folly were in somber mood. Their horses stood listless in the

84

corral near the cabin.

'You expecting your men back soon?' Hank Malloy directed his question to the man standing across from him.

'Soon enough,' Dietrich said. 'Once they have done their work.'

Dietrich was a humorless man. Broad and drifting towards being heavyset, he stared at the world through unsympathetic eyes. A thick mustache adorned his upper lip, giving him a stern appearance. In the same mold, the pair of cold-eyed men with him made no pretense at concealing their hostile stance.

Malloy glanced across at Reno, giving a slight shrug. 'I guess sending those fellers out is just his way of making sure our back trail's clear.'

Reno only nodded.

'Hell, Jack, Yarborough and Reed ain't showin', so somethin's gone wrong.'

Dietrich said, 'It's good sense to check.'

'It's taking your man a while to look

them diamonds over,' Reno said.

'There are many of them,' Dietrich said. 'It takes time. We would not want to make any mistakes. Too much has gone into this deal to have something go wrong.'

'Hell's fire, we done all right our end,' Malloy said.

'Except that you have this lawman, LeRoy, following you.'

'LeRoy's been on our backs for a while. Ain't seen him of late, but there's no other lawdog in the territory who'd stick like him,' Reno said. 'Not something we chose to happen.'

'But it has still happened, and because of that we could have more trouble.'

'You think I wanted problems?' Reno said. 'Way it's looking, I already lost two men.'

'Because they were not good enough to do their jobs.'

'They was damn good men,' Reve Donnelly said, hand slipping to grip his holstered Colt.

'Hey, let's back off here,' Reno said. 'Everybody take it easy. We're all friends. No need to get riled.'

An uneasy silence fell. The heat was unrelenting. The only one it seemed to have no effect on was Dietrich. His unmoving face showed no sign of sweat. He looked impervious to the stifling temperature.

Beyond Buckmann's Folly, the dusty sun-blasted country spread wide and empty. The brief interruption that Buckmann had created left no significant changes on the land. The rails, the water tower and the cabin would all disappear in time.

The cabin door opened and Dietrich's diamond expert stepped outside, eyes squinting against the hot glare of the sun. He was middle-aged, pale with thinning hair and slightly hunched shoulders from spending so much time bent over his work bench. He made no attempt to hide his displeasure at the harsh southwest climate.

'You done, Spearman?' Dietrich said.

Spearman mopped his sweating face. 'Done? Of course I'm not done. You don't realize how time-consuming my work is. Checking every one of those stones takes time. A great deal of time. Dietrich, you know I can't make any mistakes. Our principal won't take it lightly if he finds out he's been duped.'

For once Dietrich's mask slipped, and he allowed a momentary scowl to cross his face. He made a dismissive gesture in Spearman's direction. 'Go and do your work, then.'

'Please give me some fresh coffee,' Spearman said.

When Spearman and his mug of coffee had returned to the shack, Reno moved away from the abandoned water tower. 'Just remember we done what you asked. That satchel I delivered is untouched. Don't make the mistake of even suggesting there's any problem with those damn diamonds.'

'Mister Reno, I assure you nothing is further from my mind. As soon as

Spearman validates the authenticity of those diamonds, you will receive your money and we can all be on our way.' He poured himself fresh coffee from the pot standing by the fire. 'My principal is a man who values honesty in business dealings. There may be more work, as you have succeeded in completing this current assignment. He has plans that involve this territory, and he will need men who know it. You appear to have the correct attributes. Believe me, Mister Reno, working for my employer could be extremely profitable. A decided improvement on your old ways of riding in the shadows and stealing small.'

'Good to hear,' Reno said.

He rejoined his two partners who were standing by the old water tower. Malloy was casually rolling himself a cigarette, his nimble fingers going through the motions even as he expertly worked the tobacco into the strip of brown paper, moistened it and placed it between his lips. Reeve Donnelly helped himself to water from one of the canteens he had filled from the spring. The liquid was cool against his dry lips.

'You figure this yahoo is talking straight?' Donnelly said. 'Maybe he's foolin' with us.'

'Can't see what he'd get from that,' Reno said.

'Just don't go turnin' your back on him, and make damn sure you count that cash when he hands it over,' Malloy said. 'All I got to say.'

'Hank, you're a damn suspicious feller,' Reno said. 'There anyone you really trust?'

'On'y you, Jack.'

Reno managed a crooked grin at that.

'You forgettin' me?' Donnelly said.

Malloy gave him a slow look over as he struck a Lucifer with his thumbnail and lit his cigarette. 'I ain't ever likely to forget you, partner.'

Donnelly considered what Malloy had said. His expression brought a slow chuckle from Reno. Donnelly looked between the pair of them, and it slowly dawned on him that they were fooling with him. 'Sonofabitch,' he said.

*   *   *

As was often the case when the sun dropped below the horizon, so did the temperature, and LeRoy saw no gain to be had risking riding in the dark. As smart as the black was, it might easily step into a hole and injure itself. He realized quickly that there wasn't going to be much moonlight, and it would be an easy mistake to wander off track, so LeRoy made a cold camp in a dry wallow. He fastened the hobbles on the black's forelegs, ignoring the testy noise it made. The last thing he needed was the animal wandering off and leaving him afoot.

'Sorry, feller, no food tonight,' he said.

He tipped some water into his hat and let the black drink, then loosened the saddle. Dragging his coat from behind it, LeRoy buttoned it tight, slung his blanket around his shoulders, and settled down with his back to the curve of the wallow. He made sure his handguns were free in the holsters and kept his Winchester close at hand. He craved a smoke but denied himself the pleasure, aware that the smell from a lit cigar could carry a distance. It was the small things that could announce a man's presence. Until he sighted his quarry, LeRoy had no intention of giving them any advantage.

He knew for certain there were three men left in the Reno bunch, but with the appearance of the pair of strangers he had no way of knowing how many more he might have to face. That being the case, he needed to weigh up the total opposition. It was the nature of his work that changes could occur without warning. He had to adapt if and when that happened if he wanted to stay alive.

LeRoy slept until light broke through at dawn, awaking stiff and chill. He walked around until his muscles warmed up, took a strip of jerky from his saddlebag and chewed on it, drinking from the cold canteen. He was aware the black was watching him and ignored the baleful glare.

'Let's go pick up those tracks,' he said.

He tightened the cinch, then rolled his blanket and stowed it away. He slid the rifle into the scabbard, and decided to lead the horse for a while as he located the double line of hoofprints. After a good half hour, he swung into the saddle and let the black have its little jig as he lowered his weight into the leather.

'Hell, I know how you feel, but we all got our jobs to do.'

The black settled into a steady lope, LeRoy scanning the way ahead and wondering what he was going to find when he reached Buckmann's Folly. For certain it wasn't about to be a welcoming party. The wanton massacre of the Reverend Tamber's group had made that obvious. Jack Reno and his bunch were maintaining their reputation for hard dealing. Having proved they were low on the list for redemption, LeRoy made himself a promise to put an end to their killing ways. He had no intention of allowing any leeway, and to hell with allowing any kind of exceptions. The recall he had of the dead men, women and children of Tamber's train was enough to convince him that Reno and his bunch were at the end of their string.

The sun had risen, bringing another day of heat and stinging dust. LeRoy quit trying to brush himself off. As fast as he did, the dust returned, layering his clothes and his horse, and doing little to ease his mood. He soaked a kerchief and wrapped it across his mouth and nose. It worked for a while, but in the end the material was thick with moisture-dampened dust that was equally as bad as when it was dry. He pulled the kerchief off and threw it away. A couple of hours into the morning he climbed out of the saddle, wet his hand and wiped the black's mouth, stroking the horse's dust-streaked neck.

'Hoss, we both need a rest out of this heat, but I can't see anything in plain sight that's about to offer us any comfort.'

LeRoy took to walking again, partially to ease the black's burden and partially to stretch the kinks out of his legs. Sometime later, he spotted a patch of green and figured if there was greenery there had to be water in the area. He led the horse towards the small oasis. It turned out to be a clutch of brush and a few straggly cottonwoods. He saw the gleam of moisture in amongst the green; a small fissure issuing a flow of water. It came from somewhere under the ground, and over time had created a pool and a runoff. As always happened, the moisture generated plant life. It was never going to be any more than it was, but as far as LeRoy was concerned, in this parched area it was a veritable Eden.

He didn't have to point the way. The black made straight for the pool and thrust its muzzle in, drinking deeply. LeRoy moved to where the seep emerged from the earth, dropping to his knees and thrusting both hands into the cool liquid. He sluiced his face and neck, threw his hat to the ground, and used cupped hands to drench his hair, then bent over and drank. The water was surprisingly cool where it bubbled from the fissure, and was the sweetest LeRoy had ever tasted. He drank his fill, then sat back against one of the trees and rested for a time. Later he went to where the black was munching on some of the grass that grew around the pool, and took out his gear so he could clean his guns. The ride had coated them with dust, and LeRoy spent as much time as was needed to clean and lubricate them from the small can of gun-oil he carried with him. Only when he was satisfied with their condition did he sit back and work out his situation.

By his gauging, he couldn't be more than a couple of hours from Buck-mann's Folly. The abandoned railhead site had to be close now. He reckoned he could reach it by early afternoon, and found himself hoping that whatever business had drawn Reno and his bunch to the place would have kept him there.

There was the possibility Reno had concluded his deal and had moved on, yet there was also the chance he might still be negotiating his transaction. Whatever he had taken from Reverend Tamber's wagon seemed to be the catalyst for his actions. If Reno was making a delivery, he had to depend on the other party showing up. The moment he registered the thought, LeRoy reminded himself that it was more than likely the other party had already arrived. The pair of gunmen who had made the abortive attempt on his life had not been Reno's men, which suggested Reno's contacts had already shown their faces.

LeRoy's timing was tight. He reached the final stretch after a good couple of hours' riding. Aware he was getting close, he dismounted, choosing a deep depression in the terrain. There he hobbled the black, ignoring the baleful stare he got from the animal, and took his Winchester, knife in a belt scabbard, and the smallest canteen. On foot he was less likely to be seen, but he didn't discount the possibility of scouts scanning the area.

He took his time, spending much of it down on the dusty scrub-dotted ground, working his way in towards his destination. He crawled forward, feeling the dust work its way into his clothing, and recalled the cool water of the place he had last camped. It did nothing to offer him anything in the way of comfort, however, and he had to push the image out of his mind.

Flat down, with scrubby bushes his only concealment, he was able to see Buckmann's Folly. The water tower and the cabin. The smaller toolshed next to it. The sagging corral holding a number of horses standing motionless in the shimmering heat.

And six men. Jack Reno, Reeve Donnelly and Hank Malloy were standing around a fire over which a coffee pot hung from a metal hook. A little way off were three more men, all strangers to LeRoy; solid, and better dressed than Reno and his bunch. They were all well-armed, two of them carrying handguns in high-ride belt holsters and stubby double-barreled shotguns. The third man, standing slightly off from them, was a confident bull-chested individual with a hard face and a way of holding himself that told LeRoy he was the top dog. With no more information than that, LeRoy understood this was a man to be watched closely.

The door to the cabin opened and a figure stepped into view: a skinny stoop-shouldered man with a pale complexion which indicated he spent most of his time at a desk, away from sunlight. LeRoy watched this newcomer join the boss man and speak to him, though they were too far away for him to hear what they were saying. Whatever news the pale man had to deliver seemed to please the boss man. Once he had received the news, he broke into action, his arms waving as he delivered instructions.

LeRoy realized he had arrived at a crucial moment, and knew if he was going to make a move, this was the time.

* * *

'I figure the count has been finished,' Malloy said. 'Time maybe we get paid.'

Donnelly said, 'I reckon so, too; the only thing I don't know is if it'll be in cash or lead shot. Keep your eyes on those scattergun fellers.' He made sure his hammer thong was loose as he brought his gunhand close to his weapon.

'Reeve, you got a hell of a low

opinion of your fellow man,' Reno said.

'It's why I reached as old as I am. An' I aim to live a sight longer.'

Reno couldn't argue with the man's logic. Dietrich might have offered a promise of further work, but words were cheap and not always as genuine as they sounded. Until Dietrich actually came across with a genuine offer, it was going to be wise to stay on guard. It would be too late to realize a trap was in effect when it snapped shut. Reno raised his coffee mug, speaking quietly.

'Watch 'em in case Reeve has it right,' he said.

'If I see them scatterguns start to point my way,' Malloy said, 'I cut loose on those hombres.'

Dietrich turned to speak with Spearman. The shotgunners maintained their silent poses.

*   *   *

LeRoy was short on time. Knowing he had to make the most of what he did have, he took a long swallow from his canteen, then splashed water over his face. He left the canteen behind as he started to crawl away from his spot, not wanting the thing dragging from his shoulder as he edged his way around the site, taking himself in a wide circle that was intended to bring him to the corral. It would be necessary to move around the cabin to reach it, and he found himself counting off the minutes as he did. It was slow work, hot and uncomfortable, and he had to move carefully so as not to raise any telltale dust that might betray his presence.

Damned fool plan, he told himself. *Maybe I should have just ridden in hell for leather, shooting as I went, and —*

LeRoy flattened as he saw one of the Reno bunch move. It seemed the man, Donnelly, was staring directly at him. It could only have been a short time, but for LeRoy it seemed an eternity before the man looked away, head turning to stare in another direction. The marshal felt cold sweat trickling down his face.

He decided Donnelly was doing little more than observing the surrounding terrain, and hoped that was all. LeRoy waited a while longer, watching the trio of outlaws until he was satisfied they were not interested. Then he moved on, staying as flat as he could as he circled the area, finally easing his way behind the cabin. Out of sight, he was able to relax but maintained his careful progress.

He found he was faced with piles of debris that had collected behind the cabin. Abandoned piles of timber. Wooden crates, split and weathered, with spiny growths of dusty weeds. Stacks of rail ties. They gave him additional cover, and he was able to close in on the corral on the far side of the cabin, the small store shed stood nearby providing a little extra cover. Even now, LeRoy moved with cautious steps as he covered the final distance to the corral. Crouched against its rear, he saw that the opening to the enclosure was barred by a single length of timber which was thin and weathered from long years of exposure to the extreme climate, the surface split and cracked. It was not going to take much to shatter it. That was the hope, at least.

He circled the corral, staying low, so that the bulk of the horses stood between him and the gathered men. *This had better work*, he thought.

LeRoy didn't consider himself a reckless man. Situations often called for less-than-safe options, and this was one of them. If — and it was a big if — his plan worked and he scattered the horses, there was going to be confusion. He was counting on the gathered men to be taken up with recapturing the animals, and by the time they turned their attention on him, he would have the advantage. It was like the draw of the last card, the one that might gain the winning hand — or just as easily be the one that lost the game. A simple choice. In this instance, it could end his life. All LeRoy could do was see it through.

He slipped through the corral rails, crouching as he raised his rifle, aiming above the heads of the horses. They had shown little interest in his appearance up to now, simply turning their heads and looking away. LeRoy fired off two shots, the sound of the Winchester loud in the silence. The bunched horses broke into motion, heads jerking up, startled. LeRoy fired off another shot, and the animals broke away from the sudden racket. There were eight of them in the corral, and in their panic they sought to distance themselves from the source of the noise, crowding into the fence. It swayed under their combined weight, and the heavy bulk of horseflesh crashing into the weathered timber had an even better result than LeRoy had anticipated, the corral simply collapsing as the animals pushed through. Dust kicked up by the pounding hoofs created a stinging cloud. The shrill cries of the horses added to the confusion as they streamed away.

LeRoy used the moment to take down his first target: one of the men closest to the cabin, his shotgun raised swiftly as he searched for the cause of the confusion. He didn't get the chance to use his weapon as LeRoy settled his aim and put a .44-40 slug into him. It caught the man in the side of his neck, tearing a bloody path before it emerged from the far side in an eruption of red. Before the man hit the ground, LeRoy had changed positon and swung his rifle towards the Reno bunch, sending a pair of slugs thudding into Reeve Donnelly's chest as he snatched at his holstered Colt. The outlaw dropped instantly.

LeRoy heard the crackle of hastily fired weapons through the haze of dust. He was already on the move, ducking beneath the section of the corral that still stood, and flattening himself against the side of the cabin. He could hear raised voices, angry and confused. It was what he wanted and needed to take advantage of it before the men organized themselves.

★ ★ ★

'Has to be that damned lawdog,' Hank Malloy said.

He had heard the shots; had seen the horses stampede from the corral, and one of Dietrich's men go down with a flash of red as the slug ripped through his neck. Seconds later, two shots put Donnelly down, allowing him a few seconds of jerking in the dust before he died. Now Malloy snatched at his own weapon, hauling it clear from leather as he tried to pinpoint the shooter while the dust still obscured his vision.

'There,' Reno said. 'By the side of the cabin.'

Malloy swept his gun around, seeking a target. Only at the last second did he catch sight of the black-clad lawman.

'You're mine, lawdog,' he said, then felt something slam into his left shoulder, a brutal punch that shattered bone and blew a gory exit hole. The impact tilted him back and he hung against the timber of the water tower, pain already engulfing his upper body, blood streaming down his arm from the crippling wound. He didn't see Jack Reno dodge behind the tower, loosing off hasty shots at LeRoy's distant figure before he ran. After that, Malloy lost interest as he lapsed into unconsciousness. With the massive loss of blood from his wound, he never woke.

★   ★   ★

Dietrich had his revolver in his big hand as he turned to his remaining assistant. 'By the cabin,' he said. 'Move before he targets us.'

The gunman nodded, breaking to the right to circle the cabin while Dietrich took the forward move, his weapon up and ready. With his man moving around the cabin, they would have the lawman trapped between them. He could see clearly now, the dust kicked up by the stampeding horses having dissipated. In the distance he could hear them still running. There was no sign of Reno himself, so Dietrich put the man out of his mind.

This lawman was his prime concern. While he lived, he was a threat, and Dietrich did not like to be in such a position. The man had to be stopped — now — and for good. Dietrich had his orders: to collect and deliver the goods Reno had taken from Reverend Tamber. Before he could complete his task, however, he had to deal with this man LeRoy.

Dietrich figured he had allowed his man enough time. He dogged back the hammer and took a step towards the corner of the cabin concealing the lawman.

* * *

LeRoy saw Dietrich's man dart around the far comer of the cabin and understood the ploy: they were going to pin him between the pair of them. Not an enviable position to be in. LeRoy made his decision, leaning his rifle against the side of the cabin and drawing both revolvers. They were better suited to close-quarter situations and gave him a degree of flexibility.

He was out of Dietrich's sight for the moment, which gave him a little time. Dietrich was not going to step around the corner of the cabin and expose himself. He would wait for his man to show at LeRoy's back and take his shot, then make his own move.

LeRoy waited it out, figuring he had little choice. He picked up on the heavy-footed approach of Dietrich's man, took the hammer back on his right-hand Colt, and lined up on the cabin's rear corner. He spotted the man's shadow an instant before he came around the corner, his handgun firing as he set eyes on LeRoy's crouching figure. The man was fast, pistol in his hand, triggering a roll of shots in LeRoy's direction, flame and smoke spearing from the muzzle. LeRoy felt the burn as a slug tore at his side; then he was returning fire, holding his hand steady and taking that extra second to center his target. His Colt hammered out a pair of shots, close enough to almost merge into continuous sound. Dietrich's man came to a stop as the .45 slugs pounded his chest. Shock came next, then the slackness of death as he went down on his face.

LeRoy turned, dug in his heels, and pushed himself forward, knowing that Dietrich would show himself any second. He ran forward, moving at a fast pace that took him clear of the corner of the cabin, and launched himself in a headlong dive that took him past Dietrich in a blur of movement. As he landed, hitting the ground on his left shoulder, he twisted his body round and slid across the dirt on his back, both pistols seeking Dietrich.

Dietrich hauled himself to a stop, dragging himself round to face the lawman, his weapon seeking the target he wanted. He was seconds too slow.

LeRoy triggered both weapons, took

the hammers back and fired again instinctively. The pair of Colts crackled harshly, spouting flame as LeRoy hit Dietrich with as many slugs as he could. The man staggered back, his own weapon discharging its only shot at the ground. Multiple wounds to his torso blossomed with bright blood as the heavy slugs pounded home. With the last bullet from his left-hand pistol, LeRoy aimed and placed the .45 slug between Dietrich's eyes and the man toppled backwards, bloody chunks bursting from his shattered skull.

LeRoy pushed to his feet, feeling the aftermath of his headlong dive. It might have worked, but he knew he was going to suffer aches and pains for some time. He could feel the spreading patch of blood down his left side where he had caught the shot from Dietrich's man. The wound stung badly, but at least he was still able to move about.

What the hell, he decided; it was all down to doing his job. Law and order every time. He put away one of his pistols and reloaded from his cartridge belt. He hadn't forgotten the man inside the cabin, inspecting the diamonds. For all he knew, the feller could be waiting with a loaded pistol himself.

'You in the cabin — show yourself. Marshal Alvin LeRoy. I got a loaded Colt here, and I'll use it if you give me cause.'

He heard a scuffle of sound. The cabin door opened on dry hinges as the hunched figure of Spearman stepped out, arms raised. He looked terrified, eyes wide as he took in the bodies sprawled on the ground. 'I'm not armed,' he said.

'Do I take your word for that, mister? 'Cause right now, my ability to trust is kind of worn out.'

Spearman nodded vigorously.

'Down on your knees, then. Hands deep in your pockets. Just in case you decide to do something heroic.'

Spearman did as he was ordered, his gaze fixed on the muzzle of LeRoy's pistol. 'I don't like guns,' he said.

'Especially when they're pointing at me.'

'Hell, mister, should I care about your feelings? Way *I'm* feeling right now, I could put you down and walk away.'

'But all I've done is inspect those diamonds. Is that a crime?'

'Because of those diamonds, a bunch of innocent folk are dead. Men, women and kids. Slaughtered just so you miserable bastards could get your hands on a bagful of jewels.'

'I had nothing to do with that. Damnit, man, you can't hold me responsible. If those people died, they must have been in the way of — '

LeRoy moved with such speed Spearman had no chance to react. The Colt in LeRoy's hand slammed down across the side of the man's face with a vicious crack, sending him to the ground where he lay stunned. Blood welled from the ragged gash the blow had opened.

He turned and scanned the area

beyond the site. There was no sign of Jack Reno. He had gone . . . for now. LeRoy didn't fool himself into believing he had vanished for good. He would go looking for a horse before he returned to the cabin; he wasn't about to give up any prize waiting for him.

Crossing to the side of the cabin, LeRoy retrieved his rifle. He made his way to the coffee pot hung over the cookfire and helped himself to a tin cup of the brew. The hot liquid settled in his empty stomach, reminding him he hadn't eaten for some time. Searching the outlaws' possibles, he found a side of bacon and a small fry pan. Using his knife, he cut off thick slices, dropped them in the pan and set it over the flames. Next he fed fresh wood to the fire, bent over and dragged Hank Malloy's still body aside, then sat back against the water tower, downing a second cup of coffee while the bacon cooked.

As long as Reno was still around, LeRoy's manhunt was not over. If the man caught up one of the scattered horses, he would gain some advantage. The outlaw would be riding a horse without saddle or reins, food or water, but LeRoy figured he would still have his handgun. In Reno's hand, a .45 was a deadly weapon. The man had a steady hand and used a pistol with ease and accuracy. One way or another, he would return to the cabin.

When the bacon had fried, LeRoy sliced it with his knife, spearing it from the pan. He ate steadily, taking more coffee from the pot, managing to ease the hunger in his stomach.

He went through the abandoned possibles sacks and found what he was looking for: a couple of shirts. He put one aside, then cut the other into strips. Then he removed his own shirt, inspecting the wound in his side; a four-inch gash where the bullet had creased his flesh. He wadded up a piece of shirt and walked across to the spring, where he soaked the shirt and sluiced the wound, gasping at the raw pain it produced. When he was satisfied the gash was as clean as he could get it, he returned to the water tower, wadded a fresh piece of material, and pressed it over the gash. He had to knot strips of the shirt until he had enough to turn around his lean body, holding the padded cloth in place. It took a while to manage, but eventually he was satisfied. The makeshift bandage was going to have to do until he could have the wound looked at professionally. He put on the shirt he'd located and discovered it was a comfortable fit.

From the supplies he found in the saddlebags, LeRoy found ammunition the same caliber as his own weapons, and sat down to reload his pistols and top up his Winchester. He found a bundle of cheap cigars in one pouch and lit one, then sat back, working on his next move. It was simple enough. He had to take a walk back to where he had left his horse.

There was something he needed to do before that, however. On his feet,

LeRoy moved around the area and collected all the discarded weapons; rifles and pistols. He checked each body in case there were any concealed arms as well. Satisfied he had them all, he carried them across to the pool and dropped them into the water. Next he cut off a couple of lengths from one of the saddle ropes and used them to tie Spearman's wrists and ankles, sitting the man down against the cabin wall. Spearman had recovered enough to make a protest, but LeRoy ignored his feeble threats.

'Save your energy, feller. We got a long ride ahead of us once I settle with Reno. Just think about that.'

LeRoy drained his coffee, picked up his rifle, and headed out across country to get his horse. He had only been walking for five minutes when his side began to throb with pain. It was no surprise, but still an inconvenience. He changed his rifle to his other arm, pressing his hand to the bandaged wound, and was relieved there was no blood soaking through.

He scanned the landscape and saw no movement. Reno would still be out there, maybe even belly-down and watching him right now. Or he might have picked up one of the scattered horses and ridden away — but that thought faded almost immediately. Buckmann's Folly meant water, and just as important, money and diamonds. Reno wasn't about to give up on any of those things.

It took LeRoy twenty minutes to get back to the black. The horse made impatient snorts at his appearance. LeRoy jammed the Winchester into the sheath, removed the hobbles, and freed the reins.

'Quit the grumbling,' he said. 'At least you've had a better day than me.'

He took to the saddle, turned the black around, and headed back to Buckmann's Folly. As he approached, he checked out the area. The comparative flatness of the Texas landscape made it hard to hide anything. LeRoy saw no movement save the slight sway of the scant brush stirred by the restless wind. In the far distance he spotted the twisting shape of a dust devil, watching it dance back and forth until it vanished in the heat haze.

LeRoy dismounted, tying the black to a bracing strut on the water tower while he checked out Spearman. The man, with one side of his face streaked with dried blood from where LeRoy had hit him, was glaring with unrestrained hostility but kept his mouth closed tightly.

LeRoy took a long, slow look around. He saw no fresh boot prints that might indicate Reno had already made his way back. Even so, he made a thorough inspection. Caution was uppermost in his mind. Allowing his concentration to slip was tantamount to begging for a bullet in the back, and Alvin LeRoy had been surviving for too long to let that happen.

Stepping by Spearman, LeRoy pushed open the cabin door and stepped inside for the first time. Dusty windows allowed a degree of sunlight through. The interior was basic, but larger than he had realized. A double bunk against one wall. Cast-iron cook stove. A number of wooden chairs and a table. Cupboards on the wall. Everything held a layer of dust save for the table top where a black velvet cloth had been spread. LeRoy saw a large leather pouch open at the neck. Sunlight reflected off the mass of multi-faceted diamonds lying in view. There were more of the gems spread across the velvet cloth. LeRoy had no idea of the value of the hoard, but from the amount on view he guessed it had to be extremely high.

And this was why all those folk died? For a bagful of shiny rocks?

He recalled the sprawled bodies, bloody and crumpled like they didn't matter, and placed his hands flat on the table, breathing deeply as he contemplated the extreme measures some men would go to get their hands on what they considered was theirs for the taking. In his job, he had to face all types of brutal, perverted individuals who disregarded civilized behavior as they broke the law. He had figured he'd seen the worst until now.

LeRoy slid the diamonds off the velvet, back into the leather pouch, closing the mouth with the threaded thong. Its weight was substantial when he lifted it. Replacing the pouch on the table, he moved back outside. The diamonds weren't going anywhere until he was ready to leave.

He felt the rising wind the moment he stepped through the door. It lifted light dust and sent grains of gritty soil against the cabin. The water tower creaked as the breeze pushed against the dried-out, weathered timber.

To the west, the lowering sun shadowed the sky. LeRoy hadn't realized the day was slipping away. One thing he did know, however, was that he wasn't about to leave Buckmann's Folly today. An overnight stay, desired or not, was on the cards.

Jack Reno had spent hours tracking the scattered horses. By the time he had been able to slip away from Buckmann's Folly, the animals were long gone. The brief but bloody gunfight had left him the sole survivor. He might have expended time and energy ranting and cursing the turn of events that had robbed him of his partners and possibly the money due to be paid to him by Dietrich, but didn't make the effort. Things had happened, but he had survived. Reno planned to carry on that way. Yet it would be necessary for him to return to the site.

Necessary? It was vital.

Above everything, he had to have water. He was already feeling the debilitating effects of dehydration. The parched feeling in his mouth and throat was growing. Just the thought of the cool water of the spring at the folly was driving him on, forcing him to retrace the steps he had left behind on his escape. At the time it had been his wisest move. Jack Reno was not a coward, but he understood the concept of retreat when things turned against him. His men had gone down, leaving him on his own, so backing off had been his only option.

His search for the horses that had stampeded from the corral had not gained him anything. He'd seen a couple of them roaming around the landscape, too far for him to even get close. He had nothing to hand that would help, no rope, so his chances of cornering one were thin. He decided to concentrate on getting back to Buckmann's Folly.

Reno walked, taking a slow pace. Though it was late afternoon, the heat still burned. Too much effort would squeeze out any moisture remaining in his body. Dust kicked up from beneath his boots as he moved.

When the outline of the water tower showed, Reno sank to the ground, stretching out as he studied the place.

Sleeving sweat from his eyes, he took his time searching for movement. Was LeRoy still there? He might have left, taking the money Dietrich had carried — and the diamonds — leaving behind dead bodies. With all the horses gone, the lawman would have no means of transporting the dead away.

On the other hand, maybe LeRoy was still there, waiting in the hope Reno would do exactly what he was doing: returning to the folly to get to the water. That would be LeRoy's way. He was nothing if not persistent. His reputation as a dedicated lawman followed him wherever he went. There was something within Alvin LeRoy that kept him on the hunt long after others would have quit.

Well, Reno thought, *this is one man who works the same. I ain't stayed around this long by up and quitting just 'cause the day's turned contrary on me.*

He looked around and picked a likely spot where he could slide into a shallow

depression. It would offer him concealment while he waited out the rest of the
afternoon. There was little else he could
do until daylight faded, and the cover of
darkness would offer him a better
chance to reach the folly without being
seen. He had little choice. If LeRoy was
still out there, he would spot Reno
approaching in daylight. At least with
the absence of light, he might make it.
If he could get within pistol range, the
odds would be even better. He handled
a gun well. On top of being fast, he was
accurate. Extremely. He seldom missed
what he aimed at.

Settling in the depression, Reno slid
his Colt from its holster, untied his
neckerchief, and wiped the pistol down.
He added a sixth cartridge from his belt
as he thought about Malloy and
Donnelly. He had seen them both go
down under LeRoy's gun and won-
dered if either had survived. From what
he could recall, LeRoy's shots had been
on target. He made no concessions to
wounding in any confrontation. A dead

man could not fire back.

Dietrich and his pair of gunmen? Hard sons, but out of their depth in this part of the country. City folk, Reno decided, unused to the likes of US Marshal Alvin LeRoy. Reno saw them as errand boys sent to collect the diamonds. Facing LeRoy would allow them no chance at all.

Reno slid against the side of the depression, where the curve of the earth provided a degree of protection from the direct rays of the sun. Not a great deal, but enough to allow him some relief. Anything was welcome. Reno did his best not to dwell on the water he craved. So close, but it might as well have been a thousand miles away right now. He satisfied himself with the knowledge he would have access to that water once he had dealt with LeRoy. He half-cocked his pistol, spinning the cylinder, the soft click of the action satisfying his restless mood.

LeRoy, come dark I'm putting you

down. One less lawdog to have on his back.

★ ★ ★

There was no sense in staying out in the open, given that Reno could be around. LeRoy saw to the black, hobbling it close to the cabin before he moved, transferred all the supplies he found inside and hauling Spearman along as well. He secured the man's ankles to the legs of the chair he sat him in at the table, freeing Spearman's hands. With that done, LeRoy built a fire in the cast-iron stove and prepared coffee. When it was ready, he filled mugs for himself and Spearman, placing one in front of the man.

'It ain't poisoned, and it's likely to be the best you'll get for the near future,' LeRoy said.

Spearman picked up the mug and drank. LeRoy took his coffee and his Winchester. Standing to one side of the open door, he watched as shadows began to lengthen. He wasn't enjoying his situation, but at the moment he had little choice.

'You feel like talking?' he said.

Spearman said, 'About what?'

'How about that pouch of diamonds. Must be a story there.'

'There is. But a long one.'

'I'm not going anywhere.'

＊　＊　＊

A dark sweep of heavy cloud slid across the sky, speeding the twilight effect. The rising wind picked up dust, and LeRoy anticipated it was only going to get worse. The driven debris scoured the wall of the cabin and he had to step back a little to avoid being struck. Distant when he first heard, but rising in volume, he could hear the moan of the wind.

'Is there going to be a storm?' Spearman said.

'Looks that way.'

'Isn't it going to make things easier

for that man Reno? To get closer to us, I mean?'

'He'll use it.'

'Will he . . . I mean, he's going to be angry . . . '

'Reno will be coming for two reasons. To collect his money and to settle what he figures is due between the two of us.'

'And what about me?'

'I can't say how he'll be feeling about you,' LeRoy answered. 'Just figure he isn't going to be best pleased the way things have turned out.'

'My God, he'll kill us.'

'A man like Reno is likely to be unpredictable.'

'Then you have to protect me. I'm not used to this kind of thing. Damnit, man, that's your job.'

'You getting feisty isn't about to make me feel any more charitable.'

'I shouldn't be here. I was forced to come by the man I work for. I work in an office in New York. I'm an assayer. I value items and make decisions on how much they're worth.'

'You work with people who steal. Who send out gunmen and hire the likes of Jack Reno and his bunch. They left a group of families dead back there, shot to death . . . as you said, because they got in the way. And that's one hell of a thing to come out with. This feller you work for sounds like a worthless piece of trash. I'd like to hear who he is.'

Spearman shook his head, face blanched white. 'No, you don't want to hear about him, LeRoy. The less you know, the better. For your own sake. You go against him and he'll destroy you. Lawman or no, the man is unstoppable. He — '

'He's a man, Spearman. A .45 bullet will kill him just as easy as any other.'

'LeRoy, he's evil. Cruel. He has no concerns except adding to his power and wealth. He buys and sells men's bodies and souls. Women as well. He destroys anyone who gets in his way. Violence is his answer to solving problems. Understand me, Marshal, he is corruption personified.'

'Just to satisfy my curiosity, who is this top man? The one who pulls the strings?'

'Do you intend to arrest him? If you do, I wish you good luck.'

'Let me worry about that. Just give me a name, Spearman.'

'Luchino Trattori. He's the man at the top. They call him the Don. He controls a powerful criminal organization in New York. He has the power of life and death.'

'And the diamonds?'

'To add to the wealth he already has. Trattori is obsessed with it. It strengthens his power; his control over others. He craves it and will do anything to increase it. In the city, he controls the hardest of the crime groups. But he has plans to expand his reach; to spread out across the country. To do that, he needs more money. Those diamonds will buy him more influence and generate his long-term plans. He sees the West as having great potential and wants to be part of the expansion.'

'Regardless of who gets hurt along the way.'

'Life has little meaning to these people. Trattori himself gave the order to make sure no one was to be left alive to tell the tale. Those people on the wagon train . . . Reverend Tamber . . . Trattori gave the word they all had to be silenced. All of them.'

A gust of wind slammed against the cabin. Timbers creaked and rattled. The sound of the threatening storm rose in volume. LeRoy had experienced these Texas wind storms and knew how powerful they could become. Shrieking across the open land, with nothing to stop them, they could uproot trees and tear down buildings. More dirt, raised by the wind, hammered the structure of the cabin. LeRoy moved to check that the window shutters were secured.

'We'll be safe in here,' he said.

'From the storm maybe, but what about Reno?' Spearman said.

'We'll face that if it happens.'

LeRoy took out his knife and cut the ropes holding Spearman to the chair. The man wasn't about to make a break and presented little threat to him. Any threat would come from the storm — and possibly Jack Reno. 'Stay put,' he said.

'Where are you going? You can't leave me.'

'I'll be back shortly.'

He ducked out through the door, shoulders hunched and head down as he felt the wind buffet him. He crouched to release the black's hobbles, taking the reins and pulled the horse with him as he went back inside. Safer to have the animal close than left outside where Reno might steal it. He pulled the horse to the far side of the cabin, then turned to close the cabin door.

The shot came out of the swirling dust.

It came close, taking a chunk of timber from the door frame inches from LeRoy's head, peppering him with splinters. He jerked back, slamming the door and pushing the bolt home.

No doubt now. Jack Reno was near. Near enough to take a pistol shot. In LeRoy's book, that was too close.

★   ★   ★

Reno snapped the hammer back for a second shot. He was a shade too late. The cabin door closed with a thump.

Damn. He turned and pushed his way through the wind, making for the water. LeRoy would have to wait. He was trapped inside the cabin with nowhere to go. Reno dropped to his knees, scooping up water to ease his dry mouth and throat. He scooped up more with his left hand and splashed it over his face. Only after he had satisfied his thirst did he turn his attention back to the cabin, narrowing his eyes against the dust thrown around by the wind.

One way in. No rear door. The only way out would put LeRoy under Reno's gun. If the lawman wanted to get out, he had no choice. On the down side, however, LeRoy would have food and most likely water in there. He also had weapons.

And he had the diamonds and the cash Dietrich had brought. Plus he had the horse. Everything Reno required to take him to safety.

He moved closer to the cabin, fighting the wind as it pushed and twisted against him. With darkness falling fast, it was becoming difficult to see more than a few feet. Reno touched the cabin wall, easing along the rough timber. Reaching one of the shuttered windows, he attempted to peer inside through the slats, but they were too closely fitted to offer any view. He stumbled forward until he reached the closed door, and faced it, fast realizing he was no better off. He instinctively raised his Colt, then lowered it again.

No damn good. LeRoy would be set to resist any form of forced entry, his guns ready. Going in bullheaded would most likely offer a hail of shots before Reno had the opportunity to find a target. He needed a distraction. Something to occupy the lawman that would give himself an advantage.

Such as . . . ?

He almost laughed out loud when the answer came to him. Now it seemed so simple. A way to get LeRoy to quit the cabin.

Reno moved back the way he'd come. Battling the rising dust storm and the wind, he fought his way to the separate store shed yards from the cabin. Reaching it, he hauled open the wooden door and saw what he wanted: metal oil cans stored alongside other items. They held coal oil, used to fuel the cabin's lamps. Soaking the dried-out timber of the cabin would let him set a blaze that would force LeRoy outside. Reno would be waiting, ready to cut the man down. It was a risky plan, but he had little else going for him.

He felt in his pockets for a pack of

matches he carried to light his cigarettes, found them, and picked up two of the oil cans. Then he fought his way back to the cabin, stumbling under the force of the wind and crouching close to the front wall. Uncapping the oil cans, he tipped the oil out, liberally wetting the timber. With the second can he extended the oil-soaked area. Moving back to the store shed, he fashioned a crude torch from a length of wood and wound about it strips torn from an old horse blanket. He tied the bundle to the wood with a further strip of blanket, opened another can, and poured oil until the makeshift torch was dripping. At the door of the store shed, he took out his matches and struck one on the rough timber. As soon as it flared, he held it to the oil-soaked head of the torch. Strands of the blanket caught and flared, and within seconds the torch was burning well.

Reno didn't waste time. He stepped out into the swirling dust, the wind causing the burning torch to blaze heavily. Pushing against the storm, he staggered his way back to the cabin. He thrust the fiery torch against the timber wall, holding it there until the oiled wood caught. The flames flickered and then began to spread, aided by the wind. Reno thought they would be blown out by the wind, but the agitation increased the fire's hold, the dried-out wood catching quickly. Reno stumbled back as the flames grew, licking along the soaked wall, throwing off gathering heat.

*   *   *

'He's going to burn us out,' Spearman said.

Fire burned through the timber joints of the cabin walls. Smoke curled inside. LeRoy saw flames running the length of the front wall. The dryness of the wood encouraged the fire. It was a smart move by Reno, his intention to drive LeRoy and Spearman out of the cabin to where he would no doubt be waiting.

With no other way for them to go, LeRoy had to make his move quickly. The fire would engulf the cabin in a short time.

Reno wanted them out of the cabin. LeRoy would allow him that, but he was not going meekly. Behind him he heard the black snort as it picked up the smell of smoke.

'Spearman, you ride?' he said.

'What? Yes, I can ride.'

'Get up on that horse, and when I open the door, you ride him out as fast as you can.'

'Are you insane?'

'Could be. It's an easy choice. Ride out and get clear, or stay here and burn. Make up your mind, mister, else I'll take the ride myself and leave you behind.'

'What will you do?'

'Follow you and hope I can deal with Reno.'

Spearman dragged himself into the saddle and hauled up the reins. 'The diamonds . . . '

'The hell with them. As soon as I open that door, you give that black your heels. I think he's smart enough to go through.' LeRoy was hoping the black would have the sense to do what was expected of it. If not, they were still in trouble. 'Keep your head down when you go.'

He took hold of the door handle, feeling the heat searing through, and yanked it wide open. He whacked the black hard across its rump, yelling wildly as Spearman kicked with his heels. The black gave a startled cry and hesitated for a few seconds before it lunged forward and barreled its way through the open door. Smoke and dust swirled in its wake as it plunged into the gloom, Spearman screaming wildly. As the horse vanished from sight, flame burst across the open doorway. LeRoy, Winchester grasped in both hands, launched himself through, veering to the left as he cleared the cabin.

He heard shots above the sound of the storm — two, following each other close. He stumbled down on one knee, seeking a target, and framed in the fire's glare he saw Jack Reno.

The outlaw, eyes wide and staring, spotted LeRoy in the same instant. The big .45 came around, picking up on LeRoy as he angled the rifle round on line with the man's body.

Even with the rising drone of the wind, Reno's shout reached LeRoy's ears. 'The hell with you, lawdog.'

The pistol fired, the wink of flame brief. LeRoy felt the slug crease his cheek, leaving a bleeding graze.

He fired the Winchester, levering a second, then a third shot. Reno staggered under the impact but refused to go down. The outlaw's gun was grasped in both hands now, the muzzle shaking. LeRoy fired again before Reno could pull the trigger, and the Winchester's spout of flame sent the .44–40 slug on a direct line that ended as it slammed into Reno's forehead, plowing on through to lift a wedge of skull. Reno's last ever shot went into the dark sky as he toppled over on his back, slamming down hard.

LeRoy touched his fingers to his cheek and felt the stream of warm blood running down to soak his collar. Somewhere close by he heard the whicker of a horse. He peered into the falling darkness and made out the bulk of the animal. It came towards him, and he realized it was the black. He saw it carried no rider.

'Spearman?' he said, raising his voice against the wind.

Nothing.

Behind him, the flames from the cabin billowed out, throwing a bright glare against the dust storm. For a moment, the orange light showed the area, and LeRoy spotted the humped form on the ground yards away. He moved towards it, and bending over, saw it was Spearman. He had been hit by one of Reno's shots, the slug in his upper body. There was little blood, and LeRoy realized the slug had most likely gone directly into his heart, killing him quickly.

LeRoy went back to the black. It raised its head and watched him approach but made no attempt to move aside. Gathering the reins, he led the horse away from the cabin, taking them both across to the water source. He let the horse drink, dropping to his knees himself and splashing water on his face before he also drank.

The bullet tear in his cheek hurt like hell, and so did the wound in his side, but LeRoy figured he'd gotten off lightly. Everyone else involved was dead, including the folk in Reverend Tamber's train. A group of people caught up in the affair through no fault of their own. In truth, simply because they had been there at the wrong time. Jack Reno and his outlaw bunch, savage to the last, had decided to end their lives because they had been witness to the diamond delivery. Put to death so Reno could collect the cache and pass it along to Dietrich.

It was a wrong that needed to be

corrected. Back in New York sat the man who had set up the whole illicit affair. He had lost his diamonds, though he didn't know that yet; and when the news reached him, he would have to accept that and move on.

Justice had to be served, one way or another. Trattori might believe all he had lost were the diamonds and money.

He was wrong.

He was going to lose a deal more. Alvin LeRoy would see to that.

★ ★ ★

By dawn, the storm had blown itself out. The sky was clear and fresh. It happened after a storm, as if the natural occurrence had cleansed everything. LeRoy had tethered the black to the water tower again and wrapped himself in a blanket, curling up at the base of the tower where he had fallen into a deep sleep, exhaustion catching up. He woke stiff, his wounds still giving him some discomfort; but he decided if he could feel, he was still alive.

He smelled smoke. It was still rising from the remains of the burned-out cabin, drifting lazily in what little breeze there was now. On his feet, LeRoy led the horse to the water, where they both drank until they were satisfied. LeRoy dunked his head into the cool liquid, scrubbing his hands through his hair to rid himself of the gritty dust. He felt the stubble on his face; and that, combined with his wrinkled, grubby clothing, made him decide he must look a sight.

The black contented itself by grazing on the strip of grass that edged the pool. 'Glad someone has breakfast,' LeRoy said.

He drained his canteen and filled it with fresh water, then checked his weapons and reloaded them. Next he wandered across and stood looking at the burned-out cabin. It had collapsed in on itself sometime during the blaze, leaving a mess of skeletal rafters and blackened timber. Heat still rose from the debris. Somewhere in there were the diamonds. LeRoy wasn't about to go and look for them. He walked back to where the black was still chewing on the grass and went through the saddlebags, where he found a couple of strips of jerky. There was most likely food in the supplies scattered around the area, but LeRoy hadn't the inclination to go and find out. As he worked the tough meat between his teeth, he made his decision. Mounting, he took up the reins and swung the horse away from Buckmann's Folly, figuring that the place had certainly lived up to its name, and pointed it in the direction of the distant fort.

It was a fair ride, but it would be worth it. At the military outpost, he would be able to receive medical help, food and proper rest. He poked around in his dirty shirt and found a crushed cigar. Then he realized he had no matches, so he had to content himself with chewing on the tobacco. As the sun rose and it started to become hot, he called himself a fool for not picking up one of the discarded hats that had been lying around.

'Hoss, I ain't about to go back. Just have to tough it out. The both of us.'

Later, he pulled a shirt from his saddlebags and draped it over his head and shoulder. It was far from elegant, but in his current condition he didn't care.

* * *

As a military establishment, Fort Bellman was passable. It was situated around the spring that provided water, which was the reason it was in existence; and the scattering of buildings, a mix of timber and adobe, was a welcome sight to LeRoy when he rode in. It was not his first visit to the place.

He drew rein and slid from the saddle, leaning against the black. He felt weaker than he had earlier, became aware of wetness along his side. The wound had opened during his ride and was bleeding freely.

'LeRoy . . . '

He barely recognized the voice. The face was familiar. Sergeant Lew Tolliver. The man appeared at LeRoy's side, taking hold of his slumping figure.

'Kelso. McAndrews. Help this man to the infirmary. Quick as you like.'

Overcome by a sudden weakness that drained his reserve, he had little memory of what happened next.

★   ★   ★

The wound had become infected. The fort's doctor had to open and drain it a number of times. A fever came, LeRoy succumbing to the poison. It took him two days to overcome the resulting fatigue, and it was only on the third day he woke to find Laura Wakefield sitting beside his bed in the infirmary, applying a moist cloth to his hot forehead.

'Well, look at you. Awake at last,' she said. 'Alvin LeRoy, you had us worried.'

'Water,' he said. His voice was

reduced to a croak.

She filled a tin cup from a jug on the small locker beside the bed and lifted his head so he could drink. 'Fresh from the spring,' she said.

LeRoy stared at her. She looked different from the last time he'd seen her. Instead of rough clothing, she was wearing a blue dress, her hair brushed and shiny. 'Who are you?' he said. 'You remind me of Laura Wakefield, but . . . '

'You must be getting well. Humor, even.'

'I'm not dreaming, am I?'

'The wife of the commanding officer has helped me. This dress is part of her attempt to civilize me.'

'Well, it's doing a good job.'

'How are you feeling today?'

'Tired. Weak. But I'm hungry.'

'You haven't eaten for three days, so I'm not surprised. We'll see what the doctor says.' Laura started to rise, then paused to stare at him. 'Tolliver only told me a few things. I wanted to hear it from you, Alvin. That they're all dead. I suppose that sounds terrible coming from me.'

'You witnessed what they did. Why should you hide your feelings? Just remember what I told you.'

'Their time is coming.'

She remembered the expression in his eyes and knew she need not ask any more. 'I'll go and speak with the doctor. You just rest.'

LeRoy stared out the room's single window. He could see a patch of clear blue sky. For the moment he was content to simply lie there, though his mind was crowded with thoughts about the whole affair and what needed doing to finish it. As far as he was concerned, there was a final matter he had to attend to. He was in no doubt as to what that was. He also understood it would not be anything his superiors would approve of, so he had not made any mention in the telegraph message sent from the fort.

Fort Bellman was one of the few that boasted a telegraph line. It had been established for almost a year, connecting the army post to the outside world. As soon as his recovery allowed him to think straight, LeRoy asked for a message to be sent to his distant headquarters, detailing his ending of the pursuit of the Reno bunch. Over the sending and receiving of a number of messages, LeRoy had brought his superiors up to date. He was told to take whatever time he needed to recover. It was what he had been hoping for.

Sergeant Tolliver informed him that the fort's commander had ordered a troop to ride out to Buckmann's Folly to deal with the aftermath and attempt to recover the diamonds if possible.

'Al, we seem to be following you around and cleaning up after you of late. It's starting to get tedious.'

★ ★ ★

Luchino Trattori stepped back from the window of his study, a frown creasing his broad face. Rain streamed down the glass panes, dropping from a leaden, heavy-clouded sky. The downpour and the gloom matched his somber mood. Trattori had a great deal on his mind. Uppermost was the loss of the diamond cache he had been expecting from Texas.

He had been anticipating success with the gain of the large collection of priceless stones. He had plans to expand his enterprises into the western states, mainly California and Nevada, where there were limitless opportunities. His earlier excursion in Arizona with the High Grade copper mine had been thwarted, and he had lost heavily there. Despite a further attempt to recoup his hold over the enterprise, he had finally decided to cut his losses and move on with other schemes.

The High Grade business had been taken over by a woman after the death of her brother, and Trattori had been trying to have her killed so he could seize the mine. He had been in league with a woman named Beth Arling, a successful madam and saloon owner, when a man named Bodie had confronted them. He had wounded Beth; Angela Crown's brother had died as well. Sided by Bodie, Angela had proved to be too much of a problem, so Trattori had backed off, and other considerations took the place of the High Grade mine.

Trattori had a personal score to be settled with the man who had been instrumental in wrecking his deal in Arizona. Bodie. It had taken him time to track down the man hunter, and when he did, he had assigned his assassin, Silva to go after him.

Silva had few equals. He had worked for Trattori a long time and was considered to be one of the best, a craftsman who had even built his own handgun. Unfortunately, it had not saved him from Bodie. The two had clashed in the Pullman car carrying Bodie and a girl called Eden Chantry back to her father, Major Owen Chantry at Fort Huachuca. She had been kidnapped by a half-breed called Coyote. Bodie had rescued her, and after a long pursuit by Coyote and his men, Bodie had killed the outlaw. Taking a train that would return them to Fort Huachuca, Bodie had been confronted by Silva, and despite being shot, the man hunter had killed Silva.

It became a matter of honor for Trattori to have Bodie tracked down and killed. Whatever else he might be, Luchino Trattori respected tradition, and it was in that spirit he was honor-bound to have the killer paid in kind.

Trattori's second in command, a young man called Fabio, had been given the task of finding Bodie and ordering his death. During his search, Fabio had come across written reports from High Grade, especially details of Bodie's clash with Beth Arling. Beth was ambitious and enterprising. She had bought an ailing saloon in High Grade, allied herself to Raymond

Crown, and worked to profit from his desire to take over the High Grade copper mine. Her association with Raymond Crown had ended in gunfire, with him dead and her wounded by Bodie. Soon after, she had left High Grade, selling the saloon and moving further west.

Fabio's people had heard about Beth and her story, and though he was primarily seeking information on the man who had interfered with the diamond delivery, Fabio realized she had a connection to the man called Bodie. Beth admitted she wanted a chance to get even with Bodie; and Fabio's offer to assist in her latest acquisition, a saloon/gambling house in Nevada, gained her interest and cooperation. It was a twofold gesture. Trattori was looking to expand. Nevada was growing, and buying into Beth's enterprise was an easy way in. The plus side was that both Beth and Trattori had a mutual desire to deal with Bodie. Pooling their knowledge and resources would hopefully reap great rewards.

Fabio had Beth brought to the east coast to discuss the future venture. The young woman was sharp as well as beautiful, and it did not take her long to understand Trattori's desires. During the discussions they had, a connection was made between Bodie and the lawman, Alvin LeRoy. Beth maintained a line of informants who regularly fed her with information, and only recently she had learned that LeRoy and Bodie had met during an incident that involved them both. It interested Trattori. Now he had a link between the two, and he saw a possible opportunity to settle his grievance with them both. Using his own considerable lines of communication, he had tasked Fabio to follow through investigations of US Marshal Alvin LeRoy. As usual, he had come back with useful information.

The more Trattori learned about him, the more his respect grew. He saw a dedicated lawman who believed in what he stood for. Such a man would make a formidable opponent. LeRoy would not be swayed from his path, nor would he be intimidated or bought. Such a man, Trattori realized, would fight to the last.

Fabio came to Trattori's office now, a buff-colored paper in his hand. 'This has just come from our informant in Texas; he's had information from a source in Fort Bellman, where LeRoy's being treated for his wounds. It's going around the fort that there are many dead at Buckmann's Folly. The army sent soldiers to bury them. It would appear there were no survivors except for this man LeRoy.'

'The diamonds?'

Fabio shook his head. 'No mention. If the army found them, they're not disclosing anything. But I'll keep my eye out for any more news.'

Trattori showed little reaction. He leaned back in his ornate chair, letting go a deep sigh. His hands, spread out across his desk, flexed briefly. 'All that effort,' he said. 'Having these diamonds taken from Mexico and passed to that priest, Tamber. Hiring Reno and his people. And then to lose them before Dietrich could take possession. All wasted because of that damned lawman LeRoy . . . '

After Fabio left, Trattori called Beth into his office.

'How was it that a priest became involved?' she said once he'd passed on the latest information.

'He had little choice,' Trattori said. 'He'd used his position to allow him unnatural practices with his younger brethren. When his secret became known to one of my people, it was an easy thing to persuade him to help collect the diamonds after they were brought over the border from Mexico. Tamber concealed the cache in his wagon and transported them across Texas to a rendezvous with Jack Reno. After dealing with the occupants of the wagon train, Reno was to deliver the diamonds to my emissary. It went well until this cursed lawman showed up.'

'I've heard of LeRoy. A resourceful US Marshal.'

'His association with Bodie puts him at the top of the list.'

'Where are the diamonds from?'

'Gathered by various methods from a number of sources. In Mexico there are still collections of them from the days of the Aztecs, who used them for decorations of their costumes and in trade. My agents sought out these collections and collected them for me.'

'I take it by illegal means?'

'Let's say there are ways around many problems.'

Beth smiled. She understood Trattori; liked his thinking and the way he took a direct approach.

'The diamonds were brought to the border and passed to Tamber to be carried along with his religious goods,' he said.

'And who'd suspect a man of the

church? Even one of dubious practices.'

'Tamber was lucky. His transgressions were hushed up, and his gratitude came in the form of transporting something for me.'

'Very enterprising.'

'I need to consider how to complete my plans, now the diamonds have been lost. They would have made my goals much easier to achieve, but there are other ways. I believe that an enterprising young woman such as yourself could fare well as my contact in the west. Between us, we could taste some sweet success.'

'All I need is some financial incentive to help me get started.'

'Of course. You'll be well compensated for your efforts. As we seem to have a mutual concern in the form of Bodie, if we work together it'll be easier to track him down and arrange for retribution.'

It was a short time later that Beth Arling started on her return journey to the other side of the continent, as a partner in Trattori's plans and considerably richer than she had been on her arrival.

Unknown to her, as she left New York, the subject of part of her discussions with Trattori was just arriving in the city.

*   *   *

LeRoy had put up with the discomfort of the long train ride to New York by sleeping as much as he could and counting off the miles in his head as a distraction. He had not informed his superiors of his intentions and knew he would catch hell from them when he returned.

Still nursing his healing wounds, he set his mind on locating Luchino Trattori and dispensing some Western-style comeuppance when he found the man, even though he was embarking on a risky endeavor; *when* being the operative word. Alvin LeRoy was under no illusions, however. What he was

162

doing was strictly off-limits. Going after Trattori might get him dismissed from the service. He ignored the possibility.

The marshal was intent on handing out justice. Luchino Trattori was the man behind the whole affair. For a bag of diamonds, he had issued a death sentence to innocent men, women and children. In LeRoy's eyes, there had to be a reckoning.

He had learned as much as he could about the criminal gangs in New York. Armed with that information, after the train arrived he went into Manhattan's Lower East Side district where they operated. He took a room at a grubby boarding house as a base, and during the days he walked the streets, asking questions. He was risking his life and he understood that, but working unofficially, he had little choice. He found people were uncooperative; some obviously scared, others downright offensive.

LeRoy knew his questions were drawing attention, and in the end they evoked the kind of response he was expecting. He was into his third day when he was accosted by a pair of men. They were slightly better dressed than most of the locals; better fed too, by their appearance. And they moved with the assurance of people with connections.

The one in charge, confident in his surroundings, confronted LeRoy. He was lean and mean-faced, thumbs hooked in his pants as he stared at LeRoy. He wore a shiny bowler hat. 'You ask a lot of questions,' he said with no preamble.

'Only way to get answers.'

'One way to bring yourself trouble.'

LeRoy stood and faced him, having to look down as he was taller than the man.

'Now maybe we should go where we can work this out,' Bowler Hat said.

He let his partner edge closer. This one, heavier and solid, exposed the muzzle of a pistol held under his coat — a result LeRoy might have expected, so he went along with the pantomime. Bowler Hat led the way, his partner close to LeRoy, his pistol held steady. They moved along the sidewalk for half a block before Bowler Hat guided them down a narrow ally strewn with trash and the smell of decay. Reaching a small door, Bowler Hat led the way inside what turned out to be a derelict warehouse. If anything, the decay was stronger inside the walls.

'Now we have privacy,' Bowler Hat said. He turned to face LeRoy, producing a slim-bladed knife. He moved closer, the blade waving in front of LeRoy's face. His partner gave a soft snigger. The pistol into full view now; a .38 caliber revolver.

'We ain't never seen you before,' Bowler Hat said. 'And you're asking questions about someone important to us. Mr. Trattori don't take to out-of-towners pokin' into his business. So we got a problem.'

'Does he have something to hide?'

'Seems you need taking down a peg,'

Bowler Hat said.

The .38 man managed a sickly smile that exposed crooked teeth. His dark-ringed eyes narrowed as he made a decision, his pistol rising as he made to strike LeRoy. If he had pulled the trigger, he might have succeeded in putting LeRoy down. It was mistake, and the last one he ever made.

The second the muzzle of the pistol cleared him, LeRoy broke into action. He put his power into a solid punch that thudded into .38's face, snapping bone and twisting his head around, blood spraying from his distorted mouth. In the same move, LeRoy launched a kick that put the toe of his boot into Bowler Hat's groin as he made an ineffectual swipe with his knife. The force behind the kick drove the man's testicles almost to bursting point. Bowler Hat gave a shrill scream as he stumbled back, dropping his knife as he doubled over, clutching his groin, tears streaming from his eyes. He fell to his knees, his bowler slipping from his

166

head. With Bowler Hat out of the game, LeRoy turned and took hold of .38's gunhand, closing his own hand around the man's boney wrist. He twisted hard and kept on twisting until he heard bone crack, drawing a whimpering cry. There was no resistance when LeRoy wrenched the pistol from his limp grip. He pressed the muzzle against the side of the man's head and pulled the trigger without hesitation. The .38 made a sharp crack, the man dropping without a sound.

Bowler Hat, still clutching his groin, stared at his partner's motionless body, then at LeRoy. 'Jesus, you killed Ketch.'

'And there are more bullets available,' LeRoy said. 'You men here set the game up. All I'm doing is playing it by your rules.'

'You won't get out of town once Trattori knows what you done.'

'Thing is, I'm in no hurry to leave. Not until I reach your boss man and pay my respects.'

Bowler Hat rubbed his sleeve across

his mouth where he was dribbling uncontrollably. His eyes were flicking back and forth, seeking a way out. But there was no escape from the black-clad man standing over him, the muzzle of his dead partner's pistol aimed at him.

'What is it you want . . . to kill me as well?'

'Information, friend. That's all. Where can I reach Trattori? Right now. Not later. Not tomorrow. Right now.'

Bowler Hat saw his knife still lying on the dirty floor, only a couple of feet away. He blinked at the tears still flowing from his eyes due to the pain in his groin where LeRoy had kicked him. He figured out what his chances were. If he made a grab for the knife before the black clad man could . . .

'If I tell you what you want, will you let me go?' He was using the words to distract LeRoy as he inched his hand across the floor.

LeRoy didn't respond.

'Maybe I *could* help you.' His fingers scraped across the rough planks. Closer now. Very close. *I'll gut you, bucko*, he thought.

With the thought in his head Bowler Hat, through fear as much as loyalty to his employer, snatched at the knife, twisting his skinny body in a wild lunge. His fingers touched the ebony handle scant seconds before LeRoy's boot slammed down on his outstretched hand, crushing his bent fingers until they cracked, blood oozing from torn flesh. Bowler Hat screamed at the pain, feeling the weight of LeRoy's impacting foot.

'Not too smart, son,' LeRoy said. 'I saw that coming easy. Appears city boys are a mite slow.'

Bowler Hat let go with a howl of frustration, caught between a rock and a hard place with nowhere to go. When LeRoy lifted his foot, kicking aside the knife, Bowler Hat clutched his bloody hand to his chest.

'Think fast, amigo. I'm losing my patience.'

'All right, all right. Pier six. Hudson river. Boat's tethered there until late afternoon. The *Callisto*. Got guests coming tonight, so Trattori will be there. But he's well protected. You go after him, you won't get close.'

'What's special about this boat?'

'It's Trattori's gambling boat. Where he entertains important clients and holds business meetings.'

'Wasn't so hard,' LeRoy said.

Bowler Hat stared at the grim-faced man, blinking away streaming tears as he hugged his crushed and bloody hand. 'Now you can let me go. I need doctorin'. You said you'd let me go if I told you.'

'And you won't warn Trattori?'

Bowler Hat's gaze slid to one side as he said, 'No.'

'The hell you won't,' LeRoy said, and put a shot between Bowler Hat's eyes.

*   *   *

A pale mist hung over the river. It gave the impression that moored craft were floating on clouds. The air was heavy with moisture and the smell of decay. LeRoy stood in the shadows of a warehouse, studying the long shape of the *Callisto*. It was a hundred-and-fifty-foot steam-powered vessel, smoke drifting from the single funnel, painted dark blue and green and tethered to the pier, a gangplank giving access to the main deck. There was also a trio of suited shotgun-carrying men standing lookout at the bow.

LeRoy figured he would have a limited time to make his move. If clients started arriving for the gambling, his chances were going to lessen. He didn't want to put anyone at risk who had nothing to do with Trattori's illegal business.

He saw there were a number of small rowboats tied up against the pier and made his way to the spot. There he stepped down into one of the boats, unlimbered the oars, and loosened the painter. Perching on the narrow wooden seat, he slid the oars into position and pushed away from the pier. It never crossed his mind he was leaving himself open to becoming a target. It was to his advantage that the low mist helped conceal his quiet approach. He eased around the blunt stern of the vessel, bringing himself to the starboard side, where he managed to stand and reach the rail edging the deck. LeRoy pulled himself up and over the rail, then hugged the deck, pressing himself against the cabin structure.

He was improvising a plan as he eased his way along the cabin's length, and hoping he could make it work, because he needed to isolate the boat from the shore before he became too involved with Trattori's crew. Once that happened, there was not going to be much time to relax.

Rounding the bulkhead, he checked out the position of Trattori's gunmen. Since his appearance, they had moved along the deck and were now gathered at the far end of the main cabin structure, looking almost relaxed. He saw tobacco smoke rising from cigars and cigarettes. The penalty of taking too much for granted. Sure they were safe from any problems on board Trattori's boat. Too confident in the power of their employer. Who would dare to stand against Don Luchino Trattori?

LeRoy picked out the stern mooring rope looped round the capstan. He dropped to a crouch and made a swift move, reaching to slip the line from the capstan head. He had to grip the rope and drag it against the pull of the water to loosen it. It took him longer than he'd anticipated, as he had to fight the sheer bulk of the boat before the line gave enough for him to free it. Sweat broke out on his forehead as he used all his strength to combat the pull of the river, his eyes moving to check that the guards were still too occupied to look in his direction. He almost let out a yell of success when the boat rolled with the current, the line slackened, and he was able to ease it over the brass-topped head of the capstan. He let it drop free into the water.

LeRoy didn't hesitate, turning back into the cover of the cabin structure, where he moved quickly to the opposite end, again staying out of sight as he reached the bow. He stayed below window level as he picked up the murmur of voices coming from the trio of guards, and smiled at their words.

'Crew'll be coming back on board anytime soon.'

'It's gonna be a busy night.'

'Always is when the bossman invites those city bastards on board.'

'The damn fools take his cash for favors, then come back and leave it on the gaming tables.'

Someone laughed at that.

'Hell, they can't help bein' dumb.'

LeRoy, tight against the bulkhead, brushed against something, and saw it was a fire axe resting on hooks. He lifted it, feeling its solid weight in his hands. It would make things easier for him, as he wouldn't have to struggle with loosening the bow line.

'Hey, stern's drifting.'

'Stay here, Boone,' someone said.

There was a scuffle of boots on the deck. As LeRoy peered around the bulkhead, he saw two of the three men heading along the deck towards the stern, leaving the third guard at his post. He had his back to LeRoy, watching his partners. The lawman used the moment to rise to his feet and step across the deck. The axe in his hand made a couple of swings, the blade cutting into and through the bowline, severing the rope and biting into the wood of the capstan. The line broke free with an audible twang.

The remaining guard spun around, shotgun lifting. LeRoy had already moved forward to meet him, the axe swinging. The blade thumped against the man's chest, delivered with LeRoy's considerable strength. It cleaved muscle and bone, going in deep. The guard let go a terrified scream, stumbling back. Blood began to bubble around the blade. The guard slumped to the deck and lay bleeding there.

The closest of the guards let go with his own weapon, the 12-gauge booming out its sound. Too far away to be totally effective.

LeRoy palmed his shoulder-holstered Colt, dogging back the hammer as it rose, leveled it and held for a breath before he fired. The slug took the guard in the chest. He took a step back, eyes wide in disbelief as he went to the deck. The surviving man ran at LeRoy, letting go with his first shot as LeRoy dropped to a crouch and felt the wind of the buckshot go over his head. He returned fire, missing by a hair as the shotgunner turned in at the door to the cabin, firing off his second barrel as he vanished. Stray pellets clipped LeRoy's right sleeve, and he felt the hot sting as they gouged his flesh.

He drew his second Colt, and with a pistol in each hand he breached the door, ducking low as he entered the main structure. He caught a glimpse of the shotgunner ramming fresh loads into his weapon. LeRoy let go with a single .45 slug that hammered in between the shotgunner's eyes, stretching him out on the floor.

Loud voices reached LeRoy from the glass-paneled doors to his left. He hit the doors with his boot, tearing away the lock and smashing the decorated glass. As he moved forward, LeRoy caught movement, a gun firing and sending a slug that ripped a chunk of wood from the doorframe. He launched himself onto the thick carpet rolled aside, picking out a quartet of figures.

Two were clad in dark suits and wielded handguns. The wide cabin, displaying ornate and expensive furniture and gaming tables, echoed to the sound of gunfire. Slugs pounded the floor, sending ripped fragments of carpet into the air as they sought LeRoy's moving form. LeRoy ignored the offensive fire, setting himself to return shots deliberately. He caught one dark suit with a shot to the middle that folded the man at the waist, discharging his final shot into the floor.

He heard someone shouting, issuing orders, and took that as being from Trattori. Whatever he said had the effect of steadying the second gunman. He triggered a shot that struck LeRoy's left arm, high up. Certain that he had his man, the shooter took a step forward, easing back the hammer of his revolver. But he never made the shot. Extending his right arm, LeRoy fired twice, placing each slug in the man's chest. His target fell sideways, colliding with a chair and thumping to the floor on his front.

Silence fell. Gritting his teeth against the pain of his wound, LeRoy stood. He could feel blood running down his arm under his clothing. Nausea threatened to overwhelm him. He fought it off as he rose to his feet and faced the man he had come for.

Luchino Trattori. Solid build. Dark hair above his strong-boned face. Dressed in expensive clothing that befitted his status as a man of great importance. Just beyond him stood the lean figure of Fabio, the yes-man who did Trattori's bidding. His slack features a sickly white, he stood motionless, eyes fixed on the disheveled, bleeding figure facing them both. The revolvers in LeRoy's hands were pointing directly at his employer, yet Fabio understood he was also in the line of fire. He stood with his hands in clear sight, making no offensive moves. Not that he could have done anything offensive, because he was unarmed. He had never carried a gun in his life.

LeRoy's coat was open, revealing his badge, as he moved so that there was a wall at his back. 'LeRoy, US Marshal. Just so you know who you're talking to.'

'You have much to answer for, Marshal LeRoy,' Trattori said, still confident.

'I think you've got that the wrong way round, feller.'

'Have I? You forced your way onto my property, shot down my employees in cold blood . . . '

'Wrong again. I was in my hot blood.

Let's get that straight.'

'Then you should at least have the courtesy to inform me what I've done to bring about this . . . this injustice.'

'You hired Jack Reno and his bunch to intercept Reverend Tamber and his wagon train to collect the cache of diamonds you had smuggled over the border. Bad enough. But you also gave orders that no one must be left alive in that train to connect you to the crime.'

'I have no idea how you came to that entirely false conclusion.'

'Really. So the man named Spearman didn't work for you — the man you sent along with Dietrich and his gunmen to assess that the diamonds were genuine? He explained it all to me before he died. Your big scheme to expand your criminal empire out west, nothing to stand in your way. Not even the men, women and children all murdered by Jack Reno's hired guns. On your orders.'

'This is all in your mind,' Trattori said. 'Do you believe you can walk in here and accuse me? If you've heard of me, then you must realize I have the means to have you removed, discredited and stripped of your authority. I can even make you disappear if I desire.'

'Think about it, mister. I'm not someone you can scare with your threats. I wear this badge because it means I can tell you to shut the hell up and stop trying to intimidate me. It won't work, Trattori. So sit down and I'll tell you what's about to happen.'

'No one talks to me that way. I only need to snap my fingers and you become a dead man walking. You think I came to be what I am by allowing someone like you to tell me what to do?'

'You won't call in your hirelings this time, Trattori. Your guns are all dead. This boat has been freed from its moorings and right now we're floating down the Hudson. You're on your own.'

'Perhaps we need to come to some agreement,' Fabio said, speaking for the first time. He moved to stand behind his employer, an expression of benevolence on his face.

'Careful what you say, friend. You ally yourself with this man and you bring trouble on your shoulders,' LeRoy said. 'Dirt sticks, and the more you talk the thicker it's going to get.'

'I was about to suggest we work on a solution here.'

'Solution? Oh, I have one for you. Trattori is under arrest.'

Even now, Trattori's arrogance forced him to laugh in LeRoy's face. He thrust an arm forward, finger pointing at the lawman. 'This man amazes me, Fabio. Is he stupid enough to believe someone will arrest me when we step off this boat? This westerner coming here to my city and informing me I'm going be locked up . . . He still refuses to accept I am Don Luchino Trattori.'

'Hell, mister, I'll accept you got a loose mouth I'm getting tired of listening to. Quit trying to impress me with your title. I don't give a damn who you believe you are. So I suggest you sit down and stop talking before I stop you.'

The hard edge to LeRoy's words seemed to penetrate. Trattori backed away and sank down on one of the plush chairs close to a gaming table, resting his right hand on the smooth green baize cover. Despite his retreat, LeRoy could still see the defiant shine in his eyes. Momentarily defeated, he was still refusing to fully comply with LeRoy's instructions.

'Fabio, bring me a drink from my special selection.'

'May I?' Fabio asked LeRoy. 'I promise not to do anything foolish.

'I promise you won't either, son,' LeRoy said.

He watched Fabio cross the salon to a built in liquor cabinet, where he took a thick tumbler and filled it from a bottle he chose.

'I'd offer you a drink,' Trattori said, 'but perhaps fine whisky is something you wouldn't appreciate.'

'Not so much that. Just I'm particular who I drink with.'

A sneer of contempt ghosted across Trattori's face. He reached up with his left hand to take the tumbler from Fabio's slightly shaking hand. It should have come across as a warning to LeRoy. Something in Fabio's shifty expression made him turn his diverted gaze back Trattori, and he realized he had been tricked.

In the few seconds his attention had briefly wandered, Trattori's right hand slid from the table, snaking beneath the edge to emerge clutching a concealed Remington short-barreled double-action revolver. A hide-out weapon from a concealed shelf, kept there for the protection of the card dealer if things got out of hand. The weapon rose smoothly, Trattori's lips forming a defiant yell as he targeted LeRoy, pulling back on the trigger.

The salon echoed to the boom of the shot, flame and smoke erupting from the muzzle. In the sliver of time before

Trattori fired, LeRoy let his body fall to the side; yet the slug still hammered into his right side, cracking a rib and burning a hot path into his body.

Trattori pushed to his feet, screaming his rage, turning the Remington for a second shot, the chair tumbling on its side. Behind Trattori, the slender figure of Fabio had frozen, shock on his pale face. It had all happened fast, and now there was no going back.

For LeRoy, there was no more hesitating. He had allowed things to go awry, failing to check for concealed weapons, and Trattori's slug was the result. He slumped to his right knee, jerking up the guns he held, and saw the muzzle of Trattori's pistol seeking him. His thumbs dogged back the hammers, fingers easing back on the triggers as Trattori's bulk centered in his vision. He knew that Trattori was going to fire.

The salon reverberated to a sudden volley of shots. The second of Trattori's slugs clipped LeRoy's left arm, drawing blood. It was off target because LeRoy's own slugs pounded into Trattori, ripping his chest and throat and twisting him off balance. Then LeRoy fired and cocked, and fired again, not stopping until both pistols were empty and Trattori was sprawled on his back, bloody wounds streaming. Behind him, Fabio was slumped over a chair, blood pouring from a ragged hole in his neck where one of LeRoy's slugs had struck as it emerged from Trattori's back. The deformed slug had caused a fatal wound, severing a major artery. If Fabio had not been standing behind Trattori, he might have avoided being struck.

After the succession of shots, a heavy silence fell over the salon. Acrid smoke drifted in the air. LeRoy allowed his weapons to sag in his hands. He could feel blood soaking his arm and side. He was hurting all over and a weariness was engulfing him. As much as he wanted to move, he found he couldn't, so he let himself fall to the carpeted floor. He lay on his back, figuring it was as good a place to rest as any, because right then it was all he wanted to do, and to hell with making a mess of Trattori's carpet with his blood. He might have laughed at the thought if he wasn't hurting so much . . .

Two Months Later — Department of Justice — Washington

LeRoy was still recovering from the wounds inflicted during his showdown with Luchino Trattori. His left arm was in a sling and his side strapped up to support the cracked rib from the bullet he'd taken. Despite his pain, he had insisted on attending the summons to his hearing; and his earlier misgivings aside, he emerged with his reputation intact, though a little battered. The hearing had been long, involved, and became heated to a degree when witnesses LeRoy had not been expecting turned up representing his defense.

Laura Wakefield, whose testimony as

to the deaths of the occupants of the wagon train, went a long way to impress the hearing. Sergeant Tolliver offered similar evidence; he had been in the army troop that had later visited Buckmann's Folly, described the scene they'd found, and verified the discovery of the diamond cache located in the remains of the burned cabin.

LeRoy's visit to New York and his involvement with Luchino Trattori, following up on the information given to him by Spearman, had been a stumbling block at first. The Department of Justice officials had pointed out with some emphasis that LeRoy was out of his jurisdiction, and LeRoy himself could not deny that. In his own defense, he truthfully said he was simply following through the case that had originated in Texas.

No one in the room could deny Trattori's guilt. The law had been after Trattori for a number of years, but each time they closed in on the don, his lawyers, aided by the influence of powerful men — some in lofty positions themselves — were able to deflect any harm. Following Trattori's death, information began to be passed to the authorities. When the *Callisto* had eventually been boarded following its grounding on the banks of the Hudson, and the bloody scene discovered, LeRoy had been able to show his US Marshal badge; and after some delay, local marshals had showed up and taken over. LeRoy had informed them of his reasons for pursuing Trattori. That had given the local lawmen the incentive to step in and search the boat and also Trattori's city premises, something they had wanted to do for a long time. The resultant recovery of evidence, including gambling slips and ledgers that incriminated surprising names, gave the Justice Department the chance to arrest a number of officials. The Marshal's Office was well pleased with the result. Trattori's organization, leaderless and without their previous protection, was broken, its influence shattered; which encouraged witnesses to come forward. The investigation into Trattori's affairs would take a long time to complete.

Presented with the mass of evidence, the Justice Department was left with few options but to send Marshal Alvin LeRoy on his way, but not before giving him a cautionary dressing-down for stepping over the line. He was told to return home, stay within the boundaries in the future, and not expect any future excesses to be so easily dismissed. LeRoy nodded and accepted the rebuke with a degree of reticence that was unusual for him. He knew he was a lucky man.

During the hearing, when information was presented by the US Marshal's Office, a small item had aroused LeRoy's interest. It had come from one of Trattori's employees, wanting to cooperate with the authorities, and concerned a recent visitor called Beth Arling who had been talking business with him. Nothing stirred LeRoy's memory until another name was mentioned. Bodie.

LeRoy kept the connection to himself, but made a promise to let the bounty man know about the woman. It might mean something to him. It later turned out it did, and was to involve Bodie in a deadly confrontation.

On the steps outside the Justice Department building, LeRoy shook the hand of the local US Marshal chief, who offered thanks that was a hell of a lot more genuine before leaving. With Laura and Sergeant Tolliver at his side, LeRoy decided a mild celebration was in order, and the three of them hailed a cab and ordered the driver to take them to a decent restaurant. For the first time in a number of weeks, LeRoy felt the need of a decent meal.

'You'll be glad to get home,' Laura said.

'Maybe,' LeRoy replied. 'I still have to face my chief when I do. I'm expecting a tough dressing-down from him. He'll make those fellers we just left look like a passel of little old ladies.'

'If you need character witnesses,' Tolliver said, 'just call on us.'

'We'll back up anything you say,' Laura added.

'I might need to take you up on that.'

He couldn't help but notice the way Laura sat close to Tolliver, her hand resting lightly on his arm, and decided they were showing a distinct degree of affection between them.

At least one little bit of good had emerged from the affair, he decided. Which had to be welcome.

THE KILLING DAYS
CREOLE CURSE

BODIE MEETS BRAND:
TWO GUNS NORTH

BALLARD & McCALL:
TWO FROM TEXAS
GUNS OF THE BRASADA
COLORADO BLOOD HUNT
COLTER'S QUEST
TWO GUNS WEST